INSIDE STORIES

INSIDE STORIES

by

Jo Rousseau

Chatter House Press
Indianapolis, IN

INSIDE STORIES

Copyright© 2015
Jo Rousseau

Cover by Kelsey Dunning

All rights reserved.

Except for brief quotations embodied in critical articles and reviews in newspapers, magazines, radio or television, no part of this book may be reproduced in any form or by any means electronic, mechanical, or by any information storage and retrieval system without written permission from the publisher.

For information:

Chatter House Press
7915 S Emerson Ave, Ste B303
Indianapolis, IN 46237

chatterhousepress.com

ISBN: 978-1-937793-31-9

"…inside story the personal is transformed into the general, the universal. Story becomes the conscience of our communities."

Terry Tempest Williams
Listen to their Voices, 1983

Acknowledgments

Many thanks to Penny Dunning who gave me a chance to share my work, to my teachers Stanley Elkin, Tom Jenks, and Ruth Ozeki, and to my writing partner Noreen Lace for her support and advice.

Previously published stories include:

"Dead Dog Blues" *Writer's Digest Short Short Story Competition Collection* 2006
"The Temple at Ulun Danu" *Literary Imagination* Volume 5, Number 3, Fall 2003
"Home" *Printed Matter* 1993
"Iron Mountain" *Abiko Literary Quarterly* 1993

A Note to the Reader

Fiction is at the confluence of creativity and autobiography. The short stories in this collection are a combination of my own experience, observation, and imagination. What I experience, what I observe, and what I imagine are recorded as story and are played out in characters like Genvieve in "Moving to Jupiter's Moons." Genvieve has reached the age of retrospection and ponders how to hold in her memory her various faces from girlhood to crone; reviewing the artifacts of her life, Genvieve comes to consider that moment that changed everything.

My story is also played out by powerless women like Charlotte in "Dead Dog Blues," and by Suzanne in "This is my Father's Coat." These women inherited powerlessness from dysfunctional families, unlike Karen in "Misogi Harae" who was empowered by her father to seek, to learn, and to travel. It is my observations and emotional life being documented---not the events in my life. To write otherwise is to write removed, to write too distantly. I mean, for the writing to be authentic, the autobiography must bleed through the page.

Thus, it is the nature of story to house in its contents the autobiography of the teller. In "Home," memories of family stories told in my childhood are transformed by imagination and by the experience of the Viet Nam war to blossom into the story of Maxine and her brother Mickey. "Iron Mountain Baby," the story of Eugenia, comes from an Ozark Mountain legend in which one of my ancestors appears as the farmer at the end of the piece. And stories like "Guam, USA," "Theory of Love," and "Siberia" are based on observations as I was exposed to traveling in places where those stories are set.

In 1993, Mickey Pearlman published *Listen to their Voices*, a book that included her interview with Terry Tempest Williams. Tempest Williams explains that "inside story the personal is transformed into the general, the universal. Story becomes the conscience of our communities." "The Temple at Ulun Danu," and "The Ballad of Rhonda Ise" are perhaps the two stories that I find most moving. In the former, a mother struggles with the impossible task of keeping her child safe. I believe that, in this story, the reader identifies very closely with the fears of the mother. The personal in this story clearly achieves transformation to the universal. Rhonda's story, too, in "The Ballad of Rhonda Ise," achieves universal recognition (at least among women) by comingling the blood on the pink suit of Jacqueline Kennedy with the virgin blood of Rhonda Ise.

The stories in this book are intended to take the reader into a familiar world and then to ask the reader to re-evaluate that world by understanding that the story is connected to the specific autobiography, observation, and imagination of another woman, the writer. In this way, what is personal is transformed into the universal.

Jo Rousseau
January, 2015

Table of Contents

Dead Dog Blues. 1

The Temple at Ulun Danu. 6

Moving to Jupiter's Moons. 11

Iron Mountain Baby. 34

Theory of Love. 41

Guam USA.. 49

The Ballad of Rhonda Ise. 64

This is my Father's Coat. 75

Siberia. 85

Misogi Harae. 109

Home. 136

The Country of Her Most Beloved. 152

Dead Dog Blues

It wasn't until morning that Charlotte realized Jude was dead right there in her bed. It made sense now...the nudge that had failed to move him. Because Jude was lying square cross Charlotte's legs and because Charlotte was fragile, she had trouble pulling herself to a sitting position. She did pull herself up, though, dragging the dead dog with her. Jude's legs pointed toward her and his eyes looked away, through the window to the backyard he'd loved. His mouth hung open; his tongue fell comfortably into the folds of the quilt.

Poor Jude. He had been step six of her mother's twelve-step plan. Step one: transform the house for wheel-chair accessibility. Step two: pay off Charlotte's mortgage with the insurance money from her father's death. Steps three and four: set up a home business for Charlotte and find some clients. Step five: outfit the house with appliances and devices.

Devices.

The sixth step on her mother's plan was to find Charlotte a companion, thus the dog Jude. Now Jude was like all the other inanimate devices her mother had brought home. He was like a toaster that didn't work. Like a coffee pot unplugged. Like a television without cable.

But Charlotte hadn't loved those things. Hadn't talked to them. Hadn't felt their bulk or let them warm her bed. Those things hadn't loved her back. Still, he was now somehow like those things, an un-dog. And wasn't she herself sort of an un-person? Not paralyzed really. Not incapacitated...only hampered. She had an un-heart. Well, half way. It was a telepathic heart that warned her, "Stop! You're breaking me! Slow down!" A pacemaker at the age of eighteen. Charlotte's mother had already miscarried two babies, lost another to SIDS, and lost a husband too so step twelve, the final step, was a note on Charlotte's coffee pot: I simply could not bear another loss. It simply is not possible. Love Mom.

That was fourteen years ago. Her mother counted loss only in terms of what left her and not what she left.

Charlotte glanced at her clock. Eight-thirty. She heard her coffee pot click on, sputter, then begin to drip. Soon a call would come in. Charlotte ran an answering service in an age of answering machines and cell phones. Still, she had two clients: a police officer named Curt who was starting a private investigation service on the side and Sandy and Randy, a couple who enjoyed sending erotic message to each other via Charlotte. She supposed it was like having her watch them have sex. They always paid on time. Always sent something extra at Christmas.

Jude. Poor Jude. Now just another loss in the vague quagmire of losses; her dead father, her wandering mother. Dead or absent, it was all the same. Grief as common as salt. The answering machine clicked on. Charlotte only barely heard. Randy, maybe, leaving a message for Sandy about panties. Charlotte didn't look at Jude but at her own hands, which she turned over and over, and at her toes sticking out the end of the quilt. At the picture of her father, young then, an official military portrait that dominated her dresser like a beau's. He was a drinker. More precisely, a drunk. The older Charlotte got, the later her father had come home. When she was five, he came in at her bedtime, always smelling of beer and cigarettes when he leaned over her for a kiss goodnight. By the time he died, Charlotte was a senior in high school. He'd simply sailed the car off an overpass and came down on a gasoline pump that then exploded. In the newspaper photo, the Thunderbird's bumper dangled from the guardrail.

Charlotte looked at the thick posts of her bed. She'd bought yellow sheets and a quilt the same pattern as the curtains. There was a table beside the bed that held a reading lamp and a clock. The floor was bare hardwood.

Afterwards, her mother had gotten work in the animal shelter. It wasn't much and what little money she did bring home was dribbled away finding good homes for abandoned kittens or paying for insulin for diabetic dogs.

Charlotte settled back on her pillow and drifted off again. When she woke, she was at first disoriented but soon focused on her dog.

"Hey, Jude," she said, petting his head. "Hey, Jude. Poor doggy. Poor, good doggy Jude."

There was work. When she could muster the energy to move again, when it wouldn't break her heart to move, there was work. Not just the phone. Jude. She had to do something with Jude.

The hours passed under the animal's dead weight. When she was hungry, she lay back and dreamed of food. When she needed to pee, she let herself go in the bed; the warmth of her own urine was comforting, signaling that she, at least, was still alive.

By dusk, Charlotte stirred. Desperately, she gathered what little strength she had and pulled herself from under Jude. She let her feet dangle over the side of the bed. That she felt weak was neither new nor surprising but the glimpse of herself in the mirror was both. Her hair pretty much spiked around a pale face set with red eyes.

"It's time," Charlotte told Jude. She pulled the wheelchair as close to Jude's body as she could. Maybe this is what her mother had run away from—that loss that is one loss too many, that dram that tips the scale. A sorrow that finally stops the heart. Her mother had not expected Charlotte to outlive the dog.

Charlotte wrapped her arms around Jude and tried to coax his stiffening body into the chair. He was a big dog. As she heaved (she'd never be able to lift him from the floor if she dropped him), as she strained, her lack of breath staggered her. But she managed to get him precariously into the chair and move toward the front door. The back door had no ramp (a neglected step 9) so it had to be the front. And then she would wheel him along the sidewalk to the back yard. She moved slowly, watching every forward inch. She stopped, propped the front door open, and began again to move Jude forward. The threshold, a tiny speed bump, would take finesse. She judged her distance, backed to take a feeble run at the wee obstacle, pushed the wheel chair forward, and lurched as the chair caught the doorframe just enough to spill Jude onto the porch. Now, she was stuck. Charlotte pulled the chair back. She moved out to the porch. But she knew it was not possible. She simply didn't have the strength. She couldn't leave him here, a doorstop of a dog propping the door open at an odd angle. Charlotte was finding it hard to breathe. She gasped between wheezy sounds like sobs. She staggered against the porch rail.

Suddenly, he was there. Suddenly a man had come out of nowhere. He stood on her top step looking at her, looking at the dog, not sure what to do. Then, he moved forward, hoisted Jude in his arms and asked, "What should I do with him, Ma'am?"

He was, Charlotte thought at first, a dream, an apparition, the ghost of her father come to rescue her. But Jude was so substantially in his arms, his presence so palpable, that she knew he was no ghost.

"Ma'am? What do you want me to do with him?"

"I need to bury him." Charlotte pointed the way.

Without a word, this man that romance novels called only 'the handsome stranger" moved toward her backyard. Charlotte sat down in her wheelchair and scooted after him.

"Is there a shovel?"

"There." She pointed again.

She watched him dig quickly, with so much strength and vigor that it took her breath away. When he finished, he patted the grave with the back of the shovel.

"Charlotte," he said, "can I help you into the house? You're shivering." Charlotte stared at him blankly. Did she know him? "It's okay," he continued. "It's me, Randy. Remember,

Ma'am? Randy and Sandy? Let me help you in. When you didn't pass our messages…"

Randy. Had he come to complain? Terminate her service? His messages had not reached Sandy that day. Was he dissatisfied that Charlotte relayed his titillating messages with such absolute dullness? He wheeled her into her house and as quickly as he came, he was gone.

No more handsome stranger.

No more dog.

In the morning, Curt would call and she would tell him, for the sixth week in a row, that there were no messages for him.

The Temple at Ulun Danu

The drive to Ulun Danu is over a slow, mesmerizing road that winds through the Balinese mountains. It is hot and Maurissa and I blink sweat out of our eyes as our driver says "rice" or "banana" and points out tiered fields that make a kaleidoscope of color; patches of emerald and chartreuse, yellow and brown are ringed by banana or papaya trees. As we drive into the higher elevations, sudden bursts of rain surprise us, and surprise us again because they are over. Pedestrians make a steady stream along the roadside. Old women and men wear only sarongs, while young people wear western-style shorts and T-shirts. The route is dotted with thatch-covered platforms where people lounge, smoke, or eat. We stop along the road to buy bananas and a cold drink.

My eyes come to rest on Maurissa and my breath is taken away once more by the sight of her...so thin, so pale. I think in some vague way about what she's been through. I stand beside her like a human seismograph registering her reactions as though they are small earthquakes--a frown, a shrug, a watery-rimmed eye--each vibration sends a wave. Seeing her here...safe...the luck of her survival shakes me again. She'd lain on the emergency room gurney, her bare feet protruding from the white sheet that covered her. Her eyes were closed and she was motionless except for an occasional moan and a slight sideways movement of her head. The four months since then had been long and exhausting.

I'd hardly known what to say to her in the weeks she'd been home. I was afraid to say anything that would draw her farther away. It was clear that I could not save her, that I had no power; she had the power, the power to remove herself from her father, from me, and from the world with the systematic and tedious downing of pill after pill.

The Ulun Danu Temple has a trumpet tree at its entrance. Beyond the trumpet tree lays a pristine garden and lawn that stretches out to the edge of a lake where the temple has stood for hundreds of years. The mountains that surround the lake are abrupt and green and topped with misty-thin clouds. We follow a path edged with red, yellow and white flowers. It is a place that overwhelms the senses; the brain need not meddle. We are drawn, hypnotized by splendor, amazed that we have come to such a place.

The cluster of temples reserved exclusively for true worshippers is sheltered behind a stone wall that is interrupted by a magnificent gate that is strikingly like the spires and windows of the Notre Dame. The temples behind the wall are simple platforms with thatched roofs supported by unadorned, square columns. There are no images, just the offerings we've seen everywhere: small, flat baskets piled with banana and pineapple mixed with gardenias and incense.

She had expected me to find her dead the next morning, I suppose. Find her in her room as though she were only in a deep sleep, closing the door quietly behind me to allow her another hour, waiting until ten, then eleven, then deciding to wake her and realizing she was not asleep at all, not cradled in a warm and gentle slumber, not dreaming dreams, not half-opening her eyes and then settling, once more, into the hollow of her pillow.

The world is a wondrous place; I suspect she'd forgotten that.

The temple seems all but deserted when we become aware of a group of no more than seven men, women and children starting down the path behind us. Rissa and I step aside, giving them access. They walk in a loose line like an informal parade: yellow or blue sarongs, white shirts with green sashes. One man carries a fringed red umbrella on a high pole. Women and children carry offerings stacked on their heads. Another man carries bells. They pass through the gate and settle themselves on the floor of a pavilion.

Rissa had surprised us, home from school for a weekend, looking tired like any college student. Looking sudden. Looking spur of the moment as though she'd gotten in her car to go for pizza and found herself on the road home. We'd been glad to see her, of course, and thought no more than that she had missed us, had gotten homesick. She'd gone to her room and shut the door after awhile.

So drastic a measure. The shock of it. Gathering every pill from every medicine cabinet in the house--Porter's ulcer medication, a few sleeping pills, antibiotics, cold tablets, aspirins--who knows what.

It is like heaven, Ulun Danu. I can't tell you how much time passed before Maurissa and I sat in the grass by the lake's edge looking toward an island big enough only for a small pagoda. Rissa leaned back, then, lay full out in the grass.

"Mother?" Her tone is a shopping spree tone, the kind used to draw me to something she wants to buy. "Do you know anything about Robert Louis Stevenson?"

"You mean the writer?"

"Yeah. *Treasure Island*, that stuff."

"Well, he wrote *Treasure Island*. Oh, you already said that."

I look for every sign of hope in her. It isn't my imagination that there is some normal enthusiasm in this inconsequential conversation, enthusiasm that would have gone unnoticed in any other situation but in this, enthusiasm that sparkles like specks of gold dust after a year's panning.

"He's buried in Samoa. Did you know that?"

"No, I didn't. In Samoa?"

"Un-huh. He died in 1894."

"Hmmmm."

It sounded so normal, like any mother and daughter together on vacation. Had we been overheard, no one would guess the slow grinding of our internal machines, how they stopped and what effort it took to start them again. I don't know anymore what signifies, what is part of the suicidal depression and what isn't. Here she is sitting in front of me, looking normal as fried chicken, rattling on about Robert Louis Stevenson. It would be a relief if it weren't so odd.

"He was forty-four. Not as old as you."

"He was young. Well, young to die. Natural causes?"

"Oh, yes. Jungle fever, maybe. Or a stroke."

I said "natural causes." I astound myself. I said, "die." We are talking about Robert Louis Stevenson; it makes me giddy.

"He married a divorcee named Fanny who was ten years older than Robert and she already had two children."

"Odd choice." I'm keeping my hand in. Being responsive.

"I suppose. But he'd been sick as a child, most of his life in fact, and men like that marry someone willing to nurse them. Besides, she was rich."

How Rissa came to know so much about Stevenson is a mystery.

"Mother..." she starts. This tone is different. Not the shopping mall tone, but something more plaintive. The way she speaks makes me want to weep.

"What...what is it, Rissa?" I feel suddenly desperate. She spoke like someone finally crumbling in on herself, sinking back into the emotional invalid again. She seems frail. Vulnerable. Iffy.

"Rissa?"

That day, I hadn't let her sleep but had tried to wake her for dinner. We had ordered a pizza. The bottles for the pills she'd taken had been lined neatly on her dressing table, the pills poured into a candy dish, the glass of water empty beside it. I had gathered the bottles into a sandwich bag and sat with them on my lap as we followed the ambulance. Her father's eyes were wide with shock. The cars that passed us cast their yellow lights into his blank face.

"Stevenson wrote *A Child's Garden of Verses*," Rissa says, recovered again.

Yes, of course he had. I'd read them to Rissa on many occasions. We had even memorized a few. I look again at the pavilion; incense and the tinkling of bells drift toward us. It was not a conversation that brought us forward in any way. I suspect that she'd read about Robert Louis Stevenson in a *National Geographic* or *Smithsonian* that littered the day lounge of the psych ward. And, perhaps remembered it because she'd read him as a child. Still, there is something normalizing about it all.

"We'd better go," I say. "The roads get foggy in the evening."

The drive back to Sanur takes a lot longer, not because of traffic, but because the road is pitch black and full of pedestrians. Our driver squints through the headlights, down the dark, curvy mountain road, on the lookout for men leading their donkey home, women coming from the market, children playing in the little trafficked road. The darkness feels intimate inside the car. Rissa sits with one arm draped out the open window, the other hand relaxing on the seat next to me. A warm breeze carries with it the fragrance of vanilla fields. I feel at ease for the first time in months. As we drive through the sweet darkness, remnants of Stevenson's poem come back to me.

"Oh, I remember…Sing me a song, isn't it? Sing me a song, dah, dah, dah, dah lad that is gone, dah, dah, dah.and, uh, oh, yes, All that was good, all that was fair, All that was me is gone."

Rissa doesn't seem to hear. It's just as well. She rests her head on her arm, kept alive for now by the warm and fragrant breeze blowing through her long hair.

Moving to Jupiter's Moons

"Is this trash or what?" Nina stands too close making Genvieve blink. Stupid women like Nina, Genvieve thinks, middle-aged, dull, sloppy, incomprehensibly sexy, believe all old women are half-deaf. Besides, she stinks of tobacco; nicotine stains on her fingers are the same dingy yellow as her hair. The three women who make up The Lady Boxers are as alike as cigarette butts and Genvieve simply thinks of them as Nina One, Two, and Three. Genvieve's daughter, Madelyn, picked the Lady Boxers out of the phonebook.

Everyday for a week, Genvieve asked Madelyn, "When do the Green Bay Packers get here?"

"Lady Boxers, Mom." Madelyn corrected patiently each time.

"Lady Boxers, Green Bay Packers, whatever. When are they coming?"

Now Nina One bends down to look Genvieve in the eyes. "Does this stuff stay or go?" she hisses at Genvieve who turns away.

If Genvieve had the strength, she would lift the walker over her head and slam it into Nina One, knocking her to the floor so that the offending woman would look up at her instead of down.

Nina One places a dresser drawer, the last to be fetched from the cellar storage unit, in front of Genvieve. The Lady Boxers wheezed all morning, shuffling up and down the back stairs, three flights from Genvieve's apartment to the back door, then out, around, and down another flight into the basement, grasping drawer after drawer and retracing their steps setting each drawer before Genvieve for her instructions. This one holds scarves not worn since Kennedy was president, handkerchiefs with crocheted edges not used since the invention of Kleenex. Genvieve sees the silver edge of a picture frame barely visible beneath them. There are postcards, too, thick bundles of them. "Why do people save these things," she wonders aloud. "Everybody saves postcards, silly scraps of cardboard from people long dead," she mutters dropping them in the trash box without looking at them one last time.

Nina One shifts her weight to one hip and sighs. All The Lady Boxers wear pink sweatpants with a once white tee shirt with pink letters on the back advertising their company. Their logo is a pair of hanging pink boxing gloves.

"Give me a minute to look through it, will you?" Genvieve snaps.

Nina One turns and disappears through the back door of the apartment, which she leaves standing open letting the cold air of the hallway reach Genvieve sending a shiver through her. Genvieve hears Nina hit each step all the way down the three flights; then she hears the outside door slam.

For a good minute, Genvieve sits looking at the scarves in her hand without really seeing them. They haven't been worn in forty years; yet, like someone paralyzed, she isn't sure what she should do with them. The logic she'd used all the years to hang on to them suddenly seems ludicrous. There is never going to be a time when they "might come in handy." Never. There is never going to be a time when she will "think of something clever" to do them.

Genvieve is no longer sentimental about these things, so she doesn't quite understand why parting with things that should have been thrown away years ago upsets her. She drops the scarves in the box destined for the thrift shop. This exposes the photograph in the silver frame. Seeing the picture for the first time in so many years takes her breath away. It couldn't be more shocking if stage curtains opened to reveal the photograph or if an ocean wave receded to expose it. The blood drains out of her the minute she lays eyes on it. It is a portrait of her, her face as it hasn't been for a long time, looking slightly away from the camera.

The portrait makes her look snobbish, she thinks, the way her face turns away from the camera, not looking away in defiance or in shyness, but looking away like an emperor on an old Roman coin—an expression of offended nobility. Or maybe her head was half turned listening. Someone off stage. Out of the frame.

The Lady Boxers are coming to the end of emptying the apartment. Drawers and boxes from the darkest corners of Genvieve's life were dragged out, examined, disposed of. With each item, Genvieve passed judgment; this thing stays, this thing goes. Now, she picks up the photograph and wipes the silver frame on the hem of her dress. Dis-remembering had been painful, she thinks. It had taken time…many years. She had tucked the picture away, looking at it only on the anniversary of the occasion, eventually letting the anniversary slip by and finally, not looking at it at all, or hardly at all.

In the picture, it is Patterson's eyes she is avoiding. He took this picture of her. Patterson Durm. She was annoyed with him that day as she often was. Maybe what annoyed her was his fussing with the camera, setting it just so, talking to himself, sighing and clicking his tongue, taking and re-taking the picture as though he had the temperament of an artist, wiping the lens with his handkerchief. The truth was that Genvieve was perpetually annoyed with Patterson because he was beautiful…yes, he was beautiful. Not handsome. His hair was like a child's, white-blond that lay thick as raw silk threads. His nose was thin and his eyes bright blue, his hands too delicate for a man's. She hated loving someone so elegant.

Genvieve sets the photo on the table (that and her chair are the only furniture remaining in the room besides the boxes for storage and for the thrift shop) and looks out of the tall, narrow, bare window into the street that changed over the years but still remains so much the same. There was always a deli although not the same deli and a cleaner and some shoemaker or another. On the corner is a small grocery store owned by the same family since Genvieve and her husband moved into the apartment almost fifty years ago.

In the photo, Genvieve's skin is the color of boredom. Her eyes look dull. She supposes she often looked that way when she was with Patterson even though she loved him. By the end of that day and even now, she struggles to forgive him.

The picture was taken in December. The world was all black and white. She remembered that she had taken off her woolen hat at his request and her gloves too so that her pale hand could rest on the winter-black tree. But...where was the vapor of her freezing breath? Where was the raccoon collar of the coat he'd bought her that Christmas? No, not December. It was early March, wasn't it? The trees were just beginning to come to life. It wasn't December at all. How well she disremembered. It had been warmish for that time of year, and she and Patterson had gone out because of the beauty of the day, the relief it was from bitter February. And she remembered thinking that the harm of him came in gentle whispers like the teasing and unseasonably warm breeze of that day.

Nina Two's hand suddenly appears at the edge of the photo. "Store this?" Nina Two's shirt has a wet coffee stain on it.

"Don't touch it!" Genvieve says, panicked, as though the picture is suddenly hot. "You can see I'm looking at it, can't you?" Nina Two turns away without apology. Genvieve feels used to women like them. Sullen. Disrespectful. "And what's that you've got?" she calls after her.

"Just books," Nina Two's tone is matter-of-fact but her look challenges Genvieve.

"Humph! Just books she says!" Genvieve stretches out her hands as though to take them from Nina Two, but seeing her own hands in front of her, fragile, dry, brittle as Valentine roses in May, she knows she's already grown too old to bear their weight. "Set them on the table. I at least want to say goodbye to them."

Nina Two does as Genvieve asks but walks away muttering, "If you say goodbye to every damn thing in this dusty old place, it will take us another week to clear it all out."

Some of the books belonged to Charlie, of course, left un-minded for some twenty years without him to open them. The books, she thinks, aren't like his coat still hanging in the part of the closet that used to be his. The coat is Charlie's body, what she sees when she remembers the figure of him, the beautiful proportions of Charlie at twenty-five or even at forty. Yes, even at sixty. She smiles a little, picturing him with the collar of the coat turned up against the cold; the length of it falling just to meet the tips of his fingers and covering his precious rear-end: the navy color almost black to match his hair. It is the coat he'd worn every winter in the half-open dry cleaning truck he drove, picking up the soiled laundry, delivering the fresh. The books though, they are Charlie's mind. Many evenings, she and Charlie snuggled under the covers to keep warm in the cold apartment, reading to each other favorite passages from these books. *Don Quixote*: how many times did they read that! Carlyle's *The French Revolution*. They'd pour wine and toast, "The king is dead. Long live the king" when Louie was beheaded.

What good are they, these books? It is Charlie who is out of print and the books belong to anybody with the good sense to open them. Why didn't she dispose of them a long time ago? She tosses the books into the thrift store box; one among them, though, a gift from Charlie, she sets aside. Then, she picks up the books again and moves them to her storage pile.

When the front door rattles open, Genvieve knows it can only be Madelyn. She doesn't see her daughter immediately but she can hear her speak to what passes as the supervisor of the motley crew sent to disassemble Genvieve's life. Then, when she turns in the chair where she is sitting, Genvieve sees Madelyn standing in the hall where boxes are stacked to cart off to storage. It is the only way Genvieve would agree to go. Her things are *not* to be thrown out, *not* to be sold, and *not* be given away until she is finished with them, which she definitely is *not*! Not yet anyway. Her things must be kept in storage in case she needs them—wants them back. The apartment Genvieve is moving to is too small for the armoire that she begged Charlie for, too small for the silk-covered settee that they paid for over time. She can take only enough books to fill one wall of shelves, only enough china to fill the smallest of her cabinets. There is not enough wall for the seascapes and not enough floor for the rugs willed to them from Charlie's Aunt Maureen.

The three Boxers scurry around shoving the last items into boxes.

"Mother," Madelyn greets Genvieve, bending to kiss her cheek. She pulls up a crate beside her. "How has the day been? Not too painful I hope." Madelyn sighs too much and sits down too heavily, Genvieve thinks.

Madelyn just celebrated her fiftieth birthday. Genvieve is not prepared to watch her only child grow older. But, Madelyn is still youthful because she married well, never had to work hard, but is, as Charlie used to say even in Madelyn's younger days, well-tended.

Madelyn didn't want her mother to stay in the apartment during the move, didn't want her to watch. She asked that her mother pick out what she wanted shipped to Florida and follow it there soon after.

"But, how can I know what I want? This pair of shoes or that? These sets of sheets or those? The seascape or the landscape?" Genvieve argued, "I saw the place for two hours and I'm supposed to pick out a few things to take with me? How can I?"

At Jupiter's Moons, Madelyn smiled and nodded her head as the agent pointed out the safety features: an alarm next to the bed, another in the bathroom, and one in the kitchen. Grab bars, smoke alarms, carbon monoxide monitors, safety locks, panic buttons were all standard features. Wake up calls, room service, laundry service, taxi service all for an extra charge of course and wasn't Mrs. Jackson lucky to have such a generous son-in-law who had done so well?

"Painful? Well, Madelyn, there's no avoiding it." Genvieve knows that Madelyn and Ray are trying to do their best for her, but she also blames them for something she can't name. She pats her daughter's hand. "What better life to aspire to than a senior living condo in Jupiter, Florida, on the sixth floor of the up-scale Jupiter's Moons, each building named after a moon, mine being the beautiful Callisto building, with my apartment on the ocean side no less, like something from a Seinfeld episode."

"Honestly, Mom, I'm sorry this hurts you. I'm truly sorry."

"What's to be sorry? If I could, I would dance." Genvieve wiggles her walker back and forth to simulate a kind of frenzied waltz. "It isn't your fault, Madelyn." Genvieve, among other things, forgot to pay her bills and didn't realize it until the lights wouldn't go on and there wasn't any heat. She told Madelyn she didn't know whether to laugh or cry. She got her medications mixed up time and again and, more than once, she caught a frying pan on fire.

"Well, you won't have to worry anymore." Madelyn spies the photograph now resting in her mother's lap. "I've never seen this picture of you," Madelyn says picking up the photo. "Did Dad take this?"

No one had ever seen that picture except Charlie, not even Patterson. Time is running out for the telling of secrets, but this one? It is something Genvieve never talks about, never will talk about, partly because it is not possible to let the words escape into the air where she might have to breathe them forever.

"No," Genvieve says, "It wasn't your father but I can't really remember who might have taken it. It was a long time ago."

"How old were you?" It's a natural question but, to Genvieve, it feels like prying, like Madelyn is determined to get to the bottom of something.

"About twenty I think."

"The year you and Dad were married? But he didn't take it?" Madelyn persists.

"Maybe your father did take it," Genvieve lies. "Who can remember now?"

"Well, you look so pretty in this picture. So deep in thought."

Genvieve almost tells Madelyn just to take it. But, then the photo would only be of Genvieve when she was eighteen. It is much more than that.

Madelyn sets the picture down.

"Have you had any lunch?"

"How am I supposed to have had lunch? The movers took the refrigerator first thing. There isn't a crumb in the house. And I had to fight them not to take my bed!"

"They left the bed?" Madelyn cranes her neck to look through the bedroom door.

"Yes, they left the bed," Genevieve says triumphantly. "Where would I sleep if they'd taken it? As it is, I can't get anything to eat."

"You're coming home with me, Mom. Staying a few days until you're ready to take off for Florida. Your things will be all moved in by the time you get there. You really can't stay here tonight."

"I'm staying here. I still have a bed."

"We want you to stay with us." Madelyn emphasizes *want* to deny the more adamant *need*. "We won't be seeing you as often anymore."

Genvieve can tell it isn't what Madelyn intended to say. She knows Madelyn doesn't want to remind either of them, but there it is.

"What would you like to eat?" Madelyn looks down at her hands that fiddle urgently with her cell. "I'm hungry. How about the deli? You won't get a deli like Adele's in Jupiter."

"No, no, how can I go? They'll have everything mixed up. Everything that is to be given to charity will end up in Florida and all my best rugs will be given to the thrift shop. You go. Bring something in."

Thinking of staying with Madelyn and Ray "a few days" already annoys Genvieve. She would see them again, but she would never again see the apartment on 153rd Street. Besides, Genvieve hates the suburbs. It is almost more than she can bear. Madelyn and Ray live across the river in New Jersey in a big house in a new neighborhood where they have to get in the car to go buy even a pint of cream. In the mornings there, no church bells ring and no horns honk and the only sound is the barking of dogs elated to be out in the morning air. Genvieve calls it "nouveau common," but not to Madelyn's face. The lawns look as though they've been delivered from a florist's catalogue and, there it is, the lawn right outside the front door. Not the same at all as being three flights up. What's to keep the dirt from blowing right inside the house?

Madelyn gets up to go to Adele's. Genvieve can see Madelyn's cell phone finger itching to call the movers to come back and take the bed as Madelyn told them to in the first place. And, Genvieve can sense that *the talk* is not far away. Madelyn would repeat, as she had so often in recent weeks, how nice Florida is. How nice everybody is there. How she and the kids would come to visit at least three or four times a year and, between times, Calvin, Genvieve's nephew, would drop in. It isn't that her life is in this place. Her life was never anywhere but in her and in Charlie and in Madelyn. Now, in her grandchildren Ryan and Sara-Beth too. Descendants. Like a Slinky going down stairs. One generation falling into the next.

She would be alone with her thoughts then. In Jupiter. The apartment is on the ocean side of the building and there is a little balcony there—not large but big enough for a lunch table and a couple of chairs.

Genvieve suddenly realizes that the Lady Boxers must have gone out the door with Madelyn. It is normally so peaceful when she is alone, but now the memory of Patterson stirs her up, gets her thinking again about those times. Patterson was slender, and his slight build made him the target of brawnier men like Charlie. But, Genvieve always thought that Patterson had an aristocratic look, as if his ancestors hung on a castle wall somewhere in England or Germany. Patterson had the pompous air of royalty far removed from the throne; Genvieve teased him calling him Patty, as though he were among the pub-crawling Irish. He took it not at all good-naturedly. He wasn't lovable, no, not by a long shot; he was gloomy and brooding and that's what may have attracted Genvieve in the first place. She felt as though she were the one ray of sunlight, casting her warmth on his pathetically dark soul, the only one who could warm his frigid, bruised heart. It's the curse of some women to want the guy who needs them.

Adele's is just downstairs and it doesn't take Madelyn long to return with two bowls of soup and some knishes.

"I was just thinking, Madelyn, about what a good husband your father was."

Madelyn smiles setting the deli bags on the windowsill until she clears the table, setting the few remaining things back in the drawer on the floor, except for the photo which Genvieve tucks beside her in the chair. Madelyn pulls Genvieve's chair and a crate to the sides of the table and opens the bags, setting Genvieve's food in front of her.

"I had a good father. I miss him still." Charlie has been gone for twenty years. He barely retired when one day, he came in from the hot afternoon sun and complained of a headache; he simply went to lie down and never got up again. "What were you thinking about, Mom?"

"Oh, about what good care of me he's always taken. I mean, look," Genvieve sweeps her arms around to indicate the vacant apartment. "True, we never had much money. But he always planned for me. Planned that I'd be taken care of financially after he died." Madelyn smiles the whimsical smile of people spoken to of the long dead. "Your father, he never really needed me. Never needed anyone. He was the most self-sufficient man I ever knew." Genvieve looks out the window toward the dry cleaners across the street. Her neighbor, C.J. is just going in.

"He seemed that way, didn't he? But," Madelyn hesitates, "he needed you and he needed me too. He needed us to need him."

"Does Ray need you to need him?" Genvieve asks, suddenly cross.

"Ray? Good heavens, no." She laughs a little. "Ray isn't wired that way. He needs me all right, but not to need him. What he needs is someone trustworthy to raise his kids and to be the housekeeper, to rub his feet and plan his social life. He'd just as soon I never needed him! He needs me to nail down his non-working life—which is getting to be a bigger job the older he gets."

"Yes, these days, a man needs a woman to make the world seem like a habitable place." These days, she thinks, as though it was ever any different than that. Her phone rings and Madelyn, still chewing, gets up from her chair and waves her hand to indicate that she really must take this call and then moves off into the kitchen.

Had Genvieve needed Patterson to need her? Is that what gave her the power in the relationship, a power that she relished, but never had with Charlie? Patterson needed her all right. But she had not suspected how he needed her, not until the day in March when they had gone out to the park, Patterson armed with his new camera. He seemed unusually moody. He was never cheerful. Not that he was especially ill-tempered, either, but only that he was, for the most part, morose. It was such a pretty day that he decided to take out the Pierce Arrow that rarely left its spot in the garage. Patterson wanted Genvieve to take pictures of him posed against the sparkling grill of the vintage car. Had he said anything about engagement pictures? She couldn't remember anymore.

She can hear Madelyn talking on the phone and then coming back through the swinging door flipping her phone shut and tucking it into her pocket. From the look on Madelyn's face, Genvieve suspects that the time for *the talk* has arrived.

"Mom, the movers have agreed to come back and take the rest of your furniture. I know you wanted to stay here one more night, but it's Friday and they're booked tomorrow. Your stuff needs to go in the truck at the back so they can put another load in front of yours. We need to get the stuff on the truck today. They'll be heading for Florida on Monday." Madeline studies Genvieve. "Then," Madelyn continues, "the thrift store and the storage people will come get the boxes on Tuesday." When Genvieve shows no reaction, Madelyn sits down and begins to eat again. "I'm sorry things aren't the way you want them to be, Mom. I don't want to make this harder than it already is, but if we can just get through this, I know you're going to be so much happier in Florida."

Genvieve didn't see C.J. cross the street again but she knows the sound of his boots clomping up the stairs to the second floor, then to the third, and opening the door to his apartment across the hall.

"Mom?"

"Yes, I'm going to be happier in Florida. You've ordained it."

"We talked about this, didn't we? We said you don't have to go anywhere you don't want to go. You can stay right here in New York if you want to—just not in this apartment. Didn't we agree that you needed to be on the first floor or in an apartment with an elevator? You agreed that the change was a good one. The weather would allow you to be outside more and the services at the complex would be helpful to you? Didn't we agree?"

"Yes. We agreed. I'm sorry to be cranky. I'm sorry that this is difficult for me."

After a bit, the Lady Boxers come back, chatting, one still carrying a lunch bag from McDonald's. Genvieve can smell onions as Nina Three passes her. None of them look at or greet the two women for whom they work. Nina One, the supervisor, finishes a box she was working on before the lunch break, closes it, tapes it, marks it, and stacks it in the hallway with the others bound for storage.

Madelyn stands up and approaches Nina One. "What's left to do?" she asks her.

"There's stuff in the cellar. Not much. Get the trash out of here. That's about it."

"Would you mind stripping the bed? The movers will be back to take it. You can just leave the sheets on the floor in there."

"No problem."

"And, my mother's suitcases are in her bedroom. I think there are a few things in the closet. Will you pack them for her?"

"Sure."

"Along with any toiletries left in the bathroom?"

"Un-huh."

"If you don't mind, I'd like to settle up now. I need to pick up my son from a soccer game and I don't want you to have to wait for me to get back." Madelyn takes out her checkbook.

Genevieve finishes sorting the last drawer. Nina One, Two, and Three pick up everything but the photograph and the book Genvieve still holds onto. Everything else is packed in one of the boxes. The drawer is returned to the storage chest. The apartment is bare save for the chair Genvieve sits in and the round table. Madelyn settles up with Nina One and puts on her jacket to leave.

"I hope to be back before the mover's come, Mom, but I'm not sure that I will be. We don't owe them any money until they get your stuff safely to Jupiter. Will you be all right until I get back?"

"All right? Of course I'll be all right. And if I'm not? What do you suggest I do?" Genvieve folds her hands across her stomach.

"I'll be back soon," Madelyn says closing the door behind her.

The Lady Boxers say good-bye and tell Genvieve that they will leave through the cellar door after they dispose of the trash.

There she sits. It is the first time she's seen this apartment empty in how many years? A long time. At the beginning of things. Madelyn was still a baby, barely walking, still in diapers. Now the place is empty again after fifty years.

Genvieve closes her eyes. She can smell, she is sure, the cherry tobacco that Charlie used in his pipe and suddenly she can smell, too, the pungent odor of a freshly fired gun. She'd only smelled that once in her life and it had nothing to do with this room—still, that part of her brain suddenly opens like a storage drawer spilling out its contents across her conscious mind.

Patterson's Pierce Arrow alone should have put Genvieve in an upbeat mood that day in March. How perfect it was, how coddled. And Patterson's good mood too, but joyfulness expressed by Patterson got on her nerves. It was as if he had never mastered the art of happiness and threw himself about in awkward child-like poses and used his Donald Duck voice to make her laugh, which she adamantly refused to do. It was alarming when Patterson was joyful. When she had thoughts like that, she knew marriage to Patterson would be full of secrets. It was hard to account for the fact that she felt in love with him. It didn't make sense. Maybe it was just that Patterson's wife was a desirable person to be. Both his parents were dead, his mother of suicide and his father of cirrhosis. He had family money, went to the office when he felt in the mood, but the company was really run by a president and a board. He didn't seem demanding—no reason to be since the cooking and housekeeping were now and would continue to be done by hired help—and seemed, not only accepting but in fact encouraging of a degree of independence for his wife. And they loved each other, didn't they, even though Genvieve, unsure that Patterson would ever propose, had let Charlie Jackson begin to court her.

They finished with the photos that day and Patterson folded up the camera and put it in the floor of the backseat.

"I want to talk to you," Patterson said opening the door of the car for her. They always took off their shoes when he took out the Pierce Arrow and put them in felt bags kept in the car for that purpose. They rolled the windows down to let in the still warmish air of the day.

This was it, she thought. He's going to propose.

"I'm in love," he started. Somehow, to her shock, she knew instantly that Patterson wasn't talking about being in love with her.

"You're in love?" She stammered.

"Genny," he rarely called her by this diminutive. He turned her direction and took both of her hands, "I'm in love with Phillip." His eyes were riveted on Genvieve, monitoring her reaction.

She couldn't speak. It was 1947 and she had heard of homosexual men but she didn't realize, not only did she know one, she was expecting him to ask her to marry him. She knew that Patterson wanted her to look him in the eyes, but she kept looking down at his hands holding hers, his elegant hands with the meticulously buffed nails. She realized that her only reaction was a kind of speechless confusion.

"I didn't know if you'd suspected or not."

She felt as if she were choking. She felt as if, had she tried to utter a single word, something terrible would happen.

"Ask me anything!" he almost rhapsodized, "Really, I can't wait for you to meet Phillip! I adore him, Genny."

"Patterson, forgive me." She finally found her voice, but it was cracked with shock and uncertainty. "I'm really terribly confused."

"What is it, my love? I'll tell you anything you want to know."

"What are we doing together? What are you doing here with me?"

His face took on a gloom then that Genvieve was more familiar with. He put his arms around her as best he could in the front seat of the luxurious car. "Listen to me, Genny, I want you to marry me."

He had a tight grip on her and all she could do was blink into the highly-polished, hand-crafted dashboard. It wasn't that she expected this moment to be ecstatic, but she had expected it to be less complicated. Her mind was racing. It was impossible to sort out her thoughts and her brain went through a catalogue of who on earth she could talk to about this.

"I'd make a good husband, Genvieve." When he said her name, he always gave it the French pronunciation, Jon-vee-ev. "I'd provide a good life for you and you could take whatever lovers suited you."

Her vision of life as Mrs. Patterson Durm included shopping and volunteering and being respected for her graciousness as well as her wealth. At that moment, she tried to figure out a new vision, that, in reality, was not all that altered. Patterson, she realized, had never been part of the dream of marrying Patterson. It was marrying Patterson Durm she was in love with, not Patterson himself. Why shouldn't she live the life she dreamed of?

"What about Phillip?" Looking back on it, Genvieve knew the question was naïve. She should have understood what Patterson was suggesting.

He threw his head back and laughed. "No, no, my sweet! Phillip is mine. You can have lovers, but I won't share Phillip with you." He went from laughing to tears welling up in his eyes. "My life." He was addressing her. "You are my life. You will be my public life because you will be my public wife."

She sat stunned, watching as his tears twinkled in the fading light.

When she didn't say anything, he said, "I've taken a big risk, I suppose, revealing all this to you. I could have kept secrets from you forever. But, I know you love me and that I love you, and I thought maybe we could have everything we wanted. Women want a nice house, standing in society, money to spend—I can give you that."

She couldn't think. She couldn't quite absorb everything. That life she'd envisioned? Was it now only possible with a husband who...she didn't even know how to finish that sentence. Patterson loved her like a sister and she loved the life he could give her. That explained a whole lot. She'd thought Patterson only respectful, patient, if a little lacking in passion. She'd never even considered the life of a homosexual man.

She remembered thinking of the music room in his house, how the piano was never played. And, how most of the bedrooms were never slept in. And, how his real family was his servants and how she could change all that. She thought about her hands becoming as well manicured as his.

Genvieve is jolted out of her thoughts when the doorbell rings. She notices that it has gotten on towards dusk and there is no lamp to turn on. She has been sitting in the chair so long that she is stiff; getting up from the chair isn't easy. It has to be the movers coming back, she thinks.

"Just a minute," Genvieve calls, getting her walker into place and lifting herself up. The movers stream in and behind them is C.J. wiggling his eyebrows as though all moving men are irresistible. They let the movers pass on their way to the bedroom where they'd worked that morning. C.J. pulls a frown and then wraps her up in his hug the walker between them like a chaperone.

"Going to miss you, Genny-girl." C.J.'s hug is one of the most sincere hugs she'd ever felt, but she almost collapses into his embrace. He can feel her frail body sag, can feel her legs giving way beneath her. He leads her back to the chair and sits cross legged in front of her.

"You okay, Genny-girl?"

"I'm not so old, am I, C.J.?" She knows, of course, what the cavalier C.J. would say. But it isn't her age so much as her brain she is concerned about, memories flooding back to times that should have been long forgotten, forgetting things that happened only minutes before.

"You're one of those forever young types, Genny."

"I love you, C.J." Genvieve says thinking how easy that is to tell him and how hard it is with Madelyn or Ray. "I'm going to miss you."

"I'll come visit you. Send me a postcard with your new address. I'll come visit."

It all feels so awkward. Good-bye like that. Knowing he'll never really come to visit. Recalling that, for her, loss is becoming a way of life. He stays with her, watching the movers take the last sticks of furniture from the apartment.

One man returns with his clip-board. "What about that table and chair?" he asks.

"You want to come over to my place?" C.J. offers. "I've got a couch."

"You can take the table, but leave the chair," Genvieve instructs. "No, C.J., really, I just want to be alone for a minute." He gives her one last hug and follows the movers out.

It is absurd, her sitting there in the empty apartment, holding this photograph on her lap as though she were in the last scene of a movie when the screen fades to black and the credits begin to roll.

That night, she hadn't been able to think quickly through the proposal Patterson made and she didn't get the time to think about it later. The sun was going down and it was already dim in the car. The air was chilly; they didn't think to roll up the windows, they were so rapt in each other. Patterson was facing her, "I do love you," he insisted. "We could have a wonderful life." His back was to the window and he didn't see Phillip coming up to them. Genvieve didn't know the man was Phillip. She had imagined a man who looked like Patterson, genteel, aristocratic, but Phillip looked more like a sailor. He was dark and stocky with bowed legs and wild hair that gave him the look of a gypsy. She thought at first he was just a man walking down the street but he came right up to Patterson's open window and grabbed Patterson's arm.

"What are you doing! Did you tell her! Well, did you!" Phillip screamed at him. Patterson was so taken by surprise by the sudden appearance of his lover that he, at first, fled across the car seat and up against Genvieve.

"Phillip?" he said, relaxing a bit, "What's going on? Why are you so angry? Calm down."

That did seem to calm Phillip down a bit. Patterson got out of the car and moved into the park with Phillip, moving to the tree where he had taken Genvieve's picture. She could hear them, barely being able to contain their voices, keeping them in shouted whispers, but she couldn't understand what they were saying. She didn't want to know. She just wanted to get out of there, to go home, to find a way to think. It was almost completely dark now. The lights were coming on throughout the park but the car was between two street lights in a dark patch. Pretty soon, she saw Patterson striding back toward the car, his head down, intent on watching the grass pass with each long step. He came back around and let himself in the car.

"I'm sorry about that," he said. "Lover's quarrel." He started up the engine. Just as he was about to pull away, though, Phillip came across the front of the car, rounding the beautiful fenders to reach Patterson, lifted his arm straight out like an infantry soldier, and shot once into Patterson hitting him square in the temple point blank. Patterson fell sideways into Genvieve's lap. She had never seen a gun before, never heard one, and at first no blood was apparent, but when she put her hand down to touch Patterson's face, she could feel the warm, thick, liquid just begin to well up from his temple.

"Be careful, Patterson, the car! Don't get that on the seats," and then she realized or somewhere in the confusion, she must have realized. She couldn't help it. She slid across the soft calf seats smearing Patterson's blood that was beginning to saturate her dress. She opened the door and scrambled out of the car still in her bare feet. She didn't know whether Phillip would shoot again. She didn't know whether the single shot had killed Patterson. All she knew was that she needed to get out of the car. Non-sensically, she stood gaping at the open car door, at Patterson fallen over in the seat, at the blood dripping down into her handbag. Phillip was pacing in tight circles, banging himself on the forehead with his gun. He was groaning and crying as he paced and then he screamed out, shoved the barrel of the gun in his own mouth and shot once more. Genvieve shuddered and fell to the ground, overcome by the absolute horror of that moment.

  Someone called the police. When they arrived, she was still collapsed on the ground, her teeth chattering, her body shaking with grief and shock. A policeman took a short statement. Someone handed her the camera and her blood-soaked handbag. No one handed her her shoes. A policemen drove her home in a police car.

What had possessed her to develop those pictures and to dispose of all the others but this one? The picture of Patterson, smiling, leaning up against his silver Pierce Arrow, his handkerchief dapperly peeking from his breast pocket—She couldn't bear, really, to look at it. And Charlie? Those pictures didn't need to be in the house. But, this one of her just before this terrible thing happened? There's something about it, about her at that moment, as if it were the last time she were actually Genvieve Belouse—at least *that* Genvieve Belouse. It was before Patterson's dark shadow covered her forever.

For months after, she could barely eat or drink. All food seemed to remind her of Patterson's flesh, all drink reminded her of his blood. Charlie came over every day bringing her candy or flowers or books. And slowly, Genvieve came back to herself. Her revulsion for food was replaced by a deeply anchored sense of loss that would never quite go away.

She had expected Ryan to be with Madelyn when she returned but she came through the door alone.

"Mom! For goodness sakes! Why don't you turn on the lights? Sitting there in the dark like that." Madelyn flips on the harsh ceiling light. "Did the movers come?"

"No reason to turn on the lights. There's nothing to see anymore."

"Did the movers come?" she asks again.

"Yes."

"They took the table too?"

"Yes."

Madelyn comes over and leans against the window sill. "Is there anything you want before we go?"

Genvieve can't answer. She reaches down into the chair she'd been sitting in all day and picks up the small volume she'd set aside when she went through the books. It is a five by seven edition of *Romeo and Juliet*, covered in Italian marbleized paper with gold leaf edged pages. Charlie gave it to her one year on their anniversary. It had become a habit to read to each other before they went to sleep. It wasn't because the apartment was cold that they did it really, but because they enjoyed their time together reading and talking to each other about what they'd read. This was one of their favorites. Sometimes, they'd do the balcony scene.

Perhaps Charlie would have been fond of the idea of her moving to Florida.

"The kids are looking forward to us coming back for dinner, Mom. I told them I would pick up some of Adele's cream soda before we came home. She has that brand that nobody else seems to have. They still associate that soda with visiting their grandmother. I never remember the name but I'll know the label when I see it." She looks steadily at Genvieve. "I had to park way down the street. Mom?"

Genvieve stirs then. Getting her walker into place, she raises herself up. She's left her purse on the kitchen counter and both the book and the photograph will easily fit into it. Nina One left the suitcase by the front door as she promised. Madelyn moves that direction and picks up the suitcase, at the same time looking at text messages on her cell. Genvieve glances around the apartment one last time, then on impulse, opens a kitchen drawer and places the photograph inside, closing the drawer again. She slips the book into her handbag. No need to take the picture, she thinks. It's better left behind. That's all over now. That's all over.

"It's been a long day, huh Mom?" Madelyn says as she walks toward her. "But, you're going to love Florida. Just wait and see."

Madelyn helps her mother down the stairs for the last time, holding the walker in one hand and her mother's hand in the other. They make their way to the car and Madelyn settles Genvieve in the passenger seat, folds the walker and puts it in the trunk. She heads to Adele's for the soda. As Genvieve sits there, panic begins to rise in her. Her brain begins to buzz. She left the photograph! Now she has nothing of that time, that time that never really goes away. What possessed her to do that? She has to go back.

It is dark; the street light is broken. Genvieve opens the car door and pulls herself out. She is wobbling back without her walker steadying herself against the brick wall of her apartment building. She is just about back to her building when Madelyn comes rushing across the street.

"Mom! What are you doing? Where are you going?"

"I've left something. I have to get it." Genvieve wiggles her arm away from Madelyn and tries to go around her.

"There's nothing, Mom. It's empty. Everything is gone. What is it you think is there?"

"I have to go back and get it," Genvieve says frantically. "Let go of me, Madelyn, I have to go back."

"Tell me what it is, Mom, and I'll go get it. You don't need to climb those stairs. Let me take you back to the car, and I'll go get what you left."

"No," Genvieve says weakly as Madelyn turns her back toward the car. "No, I need…"

"What is it? I'll get it for you. What is it you think you left?"

What has she left? It is impossible to say. "Oh, Madelyn," Genvieve mourns as her daughter helps her get into the car again. Madelyn is standing with the car door open.

"What is it? What do you want me to get?" She opens the back door of the car and sets the soda on the floor and closes the door again. "Mother? What is it you want? I don't mind going back to get it. Honestly."

When Genvieve doesn't answer, when she sits with her head hanging low, Madelyn closes the car door, goes around to the driver's side and gets in. She starts the engine and then glances over at Genvieve. "I'll tell Ray to check the apartment when he goes back for the sheets and the chair. If there's anything there, I'll send it to you. Okay? Okay, Mom?"

Madelyn looks over her shoulder, then pulls out onto the street. "Just think," she says, "in another week you'll be in

Jupiter basking in the sun. You're going to love it. I just know you're going to love it."

Genvieve's chin quivers and reluctant tears wet her cheeks. She does not look back. The lights of the on-coming cars seem to turn night to day to night again. It is beginning to rain a little and Madelyn turns on the windshield wipers. Genvieve shifts in her seat for one last look at the apartment building that had been her life, but it is too late; the building has already disappeared. What happens next is unexpected. Genvieve suddenly feels lighter, feels as though some burden has lifted. She raises her drooping head to look at Madelyn but Madelyn stares at the road ahead. The next car that passes is like the rising sun and, in that rising sun, Genvieve sees the golden shore and bright blue sea from her balcony at Jupiter's Moons.

Iron Mountain Baby

  The train rocked as steadily as a cradle, its comforting clackity-clack a lullaby. Eugenia's head bumped gently against the high back of the brown corduroy seat as she dozed. The baby had been quiet, peacefully asleep in the seat beside her. If it weren't for the almost imperceptible rise and fall of her hand resting on her baby's back, Eugenia might believe he were already dead. The bundle could be just a little loaf of freshly baked bread, she thought, save for the trace of blood, a thin black line in the bend of his little finger, and the umbilical cord hastily and clumsily tied in her weariness and neatly bandaged with her white cotton stocking.
  The air, rushing warm and dry through the barely open window, peppered her dress with soot. Bright sun and shadow dancing across her closed lids made her think that she was dreaming. What had she intended when, barely able to stand, she had taken her canvas grocery bag from its hook and, wrapping her newborn son in a light cotton blanket, had placed him gently inside as if it were only a ham she were carrying off? She packed another bag as well, a cardboard valise, with her comb and clean rags, a change of clothes for the baby, and a bar of soap. Unable to carry more than necessities, she donned both petticoats, heavy and warm as she hurried around her room. Eugenia gladly left her plain muslin work clothes and dressed herself in the second-hand Sunday dress Mrs. Harry had given her to wear to church, a yellow cotton dress with lace at the collar.

She had stolen quietly down the boarding house steps just before first light, not looking back at the wide porch where she had sat many summer evenings talking with boarders, sipping sweet tea that Mrs. Harry kept iced. The wooden swing at the far end of the porch creaked as the morning breeze nudged it and Eugenia started, afraid she had been caught, but she did not turn, only listened a moment to the pump wheezing in the kitchen where Mrs. Harry was already making coffee. For a nickel, Mrs. Harry filled the miner's mug and dropped a jellied biscuit in his pail, then off he'd go, into the hills to the mine. Eugenia set out down that same street.

Her breath quickly became short. Five blocks from the boardinghouse to the railroad station. The houses along the street still dark. The baby heavy in the sack. Eugenia thought she might faint. Some miner finding her fallen in the street. Her baby crying. Right there in the street before she ever reached the station. Her face pale as uncooked biscuits. Her hair was damp with sweat by the time she collapsed on the bench at the station door, collapsed to catch her breath, to gather strength to buy a ticket and to stand without swaying. Was it blood she felt or merely sweat that trickled down the inside of her thigh?

What had she been thinking when she'd boarded that train in that small Pennsylvania mining town--her baby barely more than four hours old, she feeling exhausted and unsteady? She had purchased a ticket to St. Louis but, after hours of the sun's heat magnified through window glass, hours of the comforting rocking and humming roll, she arrived at Union Station too exhausted, too lethargic to step off the train into the overwhelming bustle of the crowds. She asked the ticket master to sell her a ticket to one of the mining towns further south. She was a miner's daughter she explained, and she thought she and her newborn son would feel more at home among their own kind. Perhaps Eugenia believed she could find another Mrs. Harry in Ironton or Leadwood, a woman who would give her room and board in exchange for laundering the boarders' sheets and helping with the cooking and canning. And find a man who needed his coal-dusty work clothes washed each week giving her just enough money to buy a bar of perfumed soap for her bath, rock candy, and mending thread. With lye soap, a corrugated washboard, a boiling cauldron in the alley behind a boarding house, Eugenia would fish out a work shirt with a long pole, and dumping it into a smaller tub, would scrub the tattered shirt clean.

Cleanliness was one of Eugenia's many proud and inconsequential virtues. In the summer, she washed her dress every other day so that she would always look fresh when she hurried down the steps from her room to begin mixing the biscuits for breakfast. Hers were flimsy goodnesses like obedience and punctuality; modesty and gentleness were her specialty. She was burdened with the drive to hard physical work; she was meticulous to the point of tedium, but she was admirably frugal to compensate. It was Eugenia's failings that were complicated; she lacked prowess in piety. She had no talent for prayer. Her prayers rang hollow in the night no matter how ardently she clasped her hands or how fervently she shut her eyes. She felt alone no matter how eloquently she prayed for God to be with her. When Brother McKee took her hand as she left church on a Sunday morning, he would say, *God be with you, Sister Eugenia*, and she would think, yes, God be with me. But her loneliness was not penetrated by the good wishes of Brother McKee or the casual summer evening chats on the porch of the boardinghouse. Patience to wait on God's will wore thin.

Chastity was a virtue she could have claimed then. But the ease of simple, uncomplicated chastity always dies, always withers under the strain of its preservation, always wilts with the effort to recast the woman's body from the child's. Chastity sooner or later becomes one of the troublesome virtues.

In the heat of the railroad car Eugenia unfastened the top button of her dress and dabbed at her moist breast with her handkerchief. Steady in the kaleidoscope of passing colors, the reflection of the bundle of her baby floated on the glass.

When Eugenia failed to fly down the stairs still tying her apron behind her, failed to take quick sips from the chipped china cup she reserved for herself, failed to brush back the strands of hair come loose in the kitchen's heat, Mrs. Harry, unable to rouse Eugenia with urgent knocks and concerned for what she had all along known, would take her master key to open the door to Eugenia's room: a pool of blood in the center of Eugenia's bed, a basin half full, and next to it bloodied rags. The scene would not be unfamiliar. She would find Eugenia's dresses still hanging in her closet but not notice that the canvas bag Eugenia used when she went to the market was missing. Mrs. Harry would gather the sheets, careful that no boarders should see, restore the room to its former order, close the door, lock it and wait not wholly expecting Eugenia to return.

When Eugenia's mother had left her in Mrs. Harry's care after the death of Eugenia's father in a mining accident, she had said *you must be a responsible girl, Eugenia. You must do what Mrs. Harry asks of you and you must conduct your life in an exemplary manner.* Her mother had intended to find work in Pittsburgh and then to send for Eugenia but Eugenia waited as the winter passed and then the summer. Then a letter came in her mother's neat unschooled hand: *I will never be able to bring you to Pittsburgh, Eugenia. I never will. The streets are too dirty and the factories are too hot. You must be responsible for yourself, t*he letter said. *It is best for you to stay with Mrs. Harry until your sixteenth birthday or until you find a husband,* Eugenia's mother had written. *Take care not to let a man have you before there is marriage as men are unreliable. Be a help to Mrs. Harry.* Her mother had promised to visit but had never come. At night, she would pray Dear Lord, help me be responsible for myself, help me resist temptation and not let a man take me until we are wed. After a year, when no husband was forthcoming, Eugenia had to examine the question of her responsibility for herself a bit more thoroughly. Was she, in fact, responsible for such things as her own loneliness? She wondered if there was something about her that doomed her to this horrible isolation. Was she to blame? How could she solve the problem of her loneliness? Neither Mrs. Harry nor God would answer the question for her.

The train had all but emptied when it reached St. Louis. Only a few scattered passengers boarded for the journey to Iron County. Somewhere a man smoked a cigar. Eugenia heard the quiet buzz of women's conversation several rows behind her, the kind of earnest talk of women with high collars and hats without feathers, wives of the company payroll master or the company store manager gone to the city to shop. Eugenia knew by the cadence of their soft voices that they were not the wives of men who mined iron or lead.

Somewhere on her journey, as the train slowed through small Midwestern towns, as it stopped at stations where children clung to their mother's skirts, Eugenia understood that women were doomed to fail; they were doomed to fail at the first and most important charge given to them: Responsibility for their own life signified by the preservation of their own virginity. And having inevitably and invariably failed at that, women understood that they were untrustworthy, incapable of looking out after their own welfare, weak and needy. It is a young girl's task to win the love of a man without giving him that which he most desires from her and that which she most desires to give him. It became clear to her that women always lose the first battle for control of their self--that men, that a man, even though he woos her gently, wants her to submit to him, wants her to abandon herself willingly into his hands. Every natural impulse tells her to surrender except that tiny core of social conscience. Eugenia realized that everything in her own nature had conspired against her. Her desire was called up by his strength and his blue eyes, by the way he lingered over his coffee admiring her skill at cutting biscuits, by his voice as low and rough as the mine he worked. She was stunned when her body signaled response against her will, when her effort to suppress her reaction resulted in a heated blush that he halfway pretended not to notice.

The boy who would be Eugenia's lover first saw her when he bought his nickel breakfast from Mrs. Harry. Then, standing outside the boardinghouse gates, he stopped on his way home from the mines to say *good afternoon, ma'am* and how was she doing? After a week, he opened the gates and sat on the porch steps drinking the iced tea Eugenia offered him. Within the month, he was sitting next to her on the porch swing. Eugenia's young man asked her if she would like to stroll with him as there were some pretty purple wild flowers down by the creek that ran not far beyond the railroad tracks in back of the feed store and she might like some to pretty up her room. So she walked with him. Three days and three walks later, Eugenia didn't stop him when he held on to her hand after he'd taken it to help her cross the tracks. Two weeks and fourteen walks later, Eugenia didn't stop him when he kissed her deep in the shade of a blossoming mimosa tree and two months after that she went with him to an abandoned mining shack where he had prepared a bed of thick clean straw.

It hadn't felt to Eugenia like defeat. It hadn't felt like failure and loss of self. It felt to her like the opposite of loneliness. Powerless on her own, she now had a powerful protector. Many weeks and many trips to the shack later, it felt like joy, it felt like triumph, it felt as though Eugenia had found the man who would be her husband.

When did she understand that she would throw her baby off the trestle as it crossed the Big River? Did the idea ferment in one of those dark tunnels through the Pennsylvania mountains and come to her with the light? When did she understand that she was utterly lost to goodness, that nothing could ever be made right again? To take her baby to a new town, to say the father had perished in a mine accident--to live a total lie forever and in lying retain the outward signs of virtue, even attract sympathy? Or live openly and honestly and listen to the town whisper about her--retain her self-respect by honoring the truth but lose the respect of the community. Did she understand that to avoid responsibility for the baby's life, she would have to take responsibility for the baby's death? When did she know that to hide one sin she would commit one far worse?

Eugenia shifted all but the layette from the cardboard suitcase to her shopping bag and placed the infant snugly inside thickly padding around his small skull. Had she intended to set the baby adrift on the Big River until, overcome, he would drown? Or did she have a premonition of the charity of the man who walked along the bank followed by his mule? Moments before she flung her baby off the train, did she imagine that she had transferred responsibility for her son's life to God? Did she whisper at the moment she let go the handle, God be with you?

When the ticket master came 'round again, he didn't seem to notice the absence of her baby. Eugenia smiled apologetically when she told him she had changed her mind again and please could she buy a ticket all the way through to Fort Smith?

Note: *This story is based on an Ozark Mountain legend immortalized in a song by J.T. Barton.*

> *...the more a nation modernizes, the less meaningful, the cooler, become the personal relationships. For people who live in such a modern society, love is impossible. For example, if A believes that he loves B, there is no means for him to be sure of it and vice versa. Therefore, love can not exist in a modern society--if it is merely a mutual relationship. If there is no image of a third man whom the two lovers have in common--the apex of the triangle--love ends with eternal skepticism.*
>
> Yukio Mishima, March 1966

Theory of Love

The road winds up Mount Ashi in curves so narrow that, when two busses meet, both stop and edge past each other cautiously, like strangers in a narrow corridor. Joan huddles against the cold exterior wall of the bus. She's a little queasy from the fumes and Seiji, leaning away from her on the small seat, feels almost seasick. He sways left, then right as the driver negotiates one turn after another, each time swinging closer to the shoulderless edge. Joan presses her forehead into the closed window, looking down to see if the bus really is as breath-takingly close to the sheer drop of the mountainside as it appears. Higher up, traces of snow dust the pink blossoms of the winter camellias; an occasional Buddha marks the old shogun trail, each one looking happily frozen, his stony palms powdered with snow.

Seiji and Joan wrestle their overstuffed backpacks down from the shelf a mile before the bus actually stops to let them off at the lakeside. Snow falls, disappearing into the water. Finished for the day, the ferry sleeps like an enormous floating dog, its leash loosely wound around the dock post. The ropeway to the top of the adjacent mountain is already tucked away, leaving only the thin, black lines of cable visible. Joan draws the strings of her parka hood tighter; Seiji flips up his collar and presses it into his neck.

"That's it!" Seiji yells, "There!" He points to a white, three story structure sitting snug on the side of the mountain. Joan squints. Seiji is elated that he's found the hotel so quickly. There was no address, only the bus stop name and a picture postcard verifying their reservation. The snow melts on his glasses and trickles down his face like tears of joy. To Joan, the hotel looks a mile straight up and her shoulder is already beginning to ache. She shifts her backpack to evenly distribute its weight. The noxious fumes of the bus linger in her nostrils and her tennis shoes are sponges absorbing the puddle trying to form around her feet.

The thing that Joan envies most about Seiji is his ability to eke a sense of achievement out of the smallest and most meaningless successes. He's full of pride just trudging up the steep grade of the pavement towards the hotel. When he looks back at her, she returns his smile. Seiji is handsome, lean and small-boned, average height for a Japanese of his generation. The legs of his faded jeans are snug and tuck into mountain boots that look strikingly like loaves of crusty, petrified bread. His left foot tends inward at an awkward angle as he walks.

The thing that Seiji admires most about Joan is that she seems content just to keep company with him. She'll stand patiently while he scans the landscape for the hotel and smile with him when he discovers it, she'll follow behind him along the trail that leads to the door and she'll allow him to bring her safely to the warmth and coziness of the inn. Seiji realizes Joan permits him to be leader and, for now, he plays the role happily. At moments like these, Seiji finds Joan endearingly feminine.

The hotel is large for a minshuku, eight rooms that climb up the steep side of Mt. Ashi. The blue carpet is thin and faded in spots but panoramic windows lay the beauty of the Japanese mountains and lake before them; French doors lead to tables set with pink cloths. In the ante-room, Seiji and Joan pry off their wet shoes and don slippers that line the wall. Seiji handles the registration while Joan works at her shoe laces. After two years at the University of Tokyo, her Japanese is still too marginal for the simplest task.

The door to their second floor room opens onto a bed that spans practically wall to wall, leaving only space for the door to open and a path around the bed. The bathroom is like the toilet room of a large boat, the fiberglass extruded in one fell swoop, walls, tub, toilet and floor.

Seiji uses the bathroom first. Then, Joan.

"This is okay, huh?" Seiji says testing the bed. Joan sits down on the edge. She nods.

Seiji and Joan had never spent an entire weekend together before. They'd certainly spent whole nights together during vigils, sitting on the sidewalk in front of the Chinese embassy in Moto-Azabu, protesting the genocide of the Tibetans by the Chinese, holding one candle until it burned itself out and then lighting another from the other's flame. And, they'd had sex together too, but not at the same times they'd spent the nights together. The prospect of sleeping all night together in a bed after having sex weighed heavily on them both.

What Joan admires most about Seiji is his commitment to the cause and to the group's leader, Doug Hofield. Her own commitment falls far short of Seiji's. She'd skip meetings of the Free Tibet Society to study for exams and she'd go back to her apartment after putting in only a couple of hours at a vigil and she'd leave early if she was cold or if it started to mist. But Seiji, one of the few Japanese in the otherwise Western group, always stayed to the last man. As long as Doug stayed, there was Seiji beside him smiling as if they were sharing masculine secrets, were doing something brave, or daring, even a little dangerous and enjoying every minute of it. Then, they said boku between them.

Seiji watches Joan sitting on the side of the bed and he wishes that he felt like kissing her but he doesn't. He doesn't know why he doesn't feel like it. Her hair, he is thinking, lacks the bounce it has when she just finishes washing it and, really, he prefers girls with slimmer hips. Joan is sitting on the edge of the bed, bouncing lightly as though trying with all her might to come up with an opinion on whether the bed is comfortable. It strikes Seiji that Joan is overwhelmed with trying to discover what criteria might be appropriate to use, what measures, and how to communicate them. Wine is discussed in terms of bouquet and fullness, but how is one to discuss the qualities and degrees of comfort of a mattress? Joan stops bouncing.

What seriously bothers Seiji about Joan, bothers him much more than the dullness of her hair or the wideness of her American hips, is that she never seems to have any opinions. Doug had mentioned it too. Seiji isn't sure that Joan doesn't walk around in a continual daze. Joan's grades are good, that's true enough--she isn't stupid-- but, as Doug pointed out, there is a big difference between the ability to mentally process textbook information and genuine thinking. That's what Seiji finds so stimulating about the Free Tibet Society and about Doug. Doug really knows how to think! Joan is a follower.

Joan and Seiji had made a good team that semester. Doug had asked them to produce posters for a campus information booth. Tables were set up along the walkway around the library. Seiji had designed the posters and Joan had done artwork that fulfilled Seiji's vision far better than he could have himself. They had presented the posters to Doug who had praised them lavishly. Seiji had puffed up, proud of their work and he had flung his arm around Joan and given her a hard hug to celebrate their success. Joan had smiled, believing Doug was making far too much of their effort. Seiji and Joan had had remarkable sex that evening. It was as though the symbiosis that had produced the posters was still at work for them, connecting them almost spiritually. And, good sex had made Seiji proud in the same way the posters had, as though he and Joan were masters of life, as though they were again worthy of Doug's praise.

If the snow kept falling, the boats wouldn't run the next day; Joan had brought her art history book. She has an exam on Monday but she doesn't want to be the first to blatantly withdraw her attention from her companion. She waits for him to signal that he wants to be relieved of her attention. She isn't sure what the signal will be but she knows she will sense when Seiji will approve, even welcome, her drawing out her book. While she senses these things, Seiji never seems aware.

In fact, what Joan dislikes most about Seiji is that he seems absolutely unable to fathom how and what she thinks. He doesn't understand that what he chalks up merely to good chemistry between them is actually due to her awareness and sense of timing. Nor does he appreciate that what he assesses as her inherently passive and feminine nature is really a willing concession to his ego. Still, his dark thick hair and his tight body, stretched out now on the bed in an expression of latent energy, appeal to Joan. She remembers seeing Seiji standing with Doug, each of them holding a bundle of white candles to be handed out. Here was a man capable of single-minded devotion, she thought. Here was a man whose concerns expand beyond himself to those countries, people, and situations he'd only heard about.

Her involvement with the group, she knew quite well, was not a concern for the Tibetan people--that had come later. Joan was drawn into the group by the magnetic Doug Hofield. Laidback and assured, Doug's every movement suggested confidence and leadership. In the Japanese literature class where they'd met, Doug's literary insights had kept her in awe. When he'd asked her to attend a meeting of the Free Tibet Society, it was impossible for her to refuse. Often, Doug, Joan, and Seiji whiled away the hours after a meeting, discussing America or Japan or Tibet and drinking wine at an Italian restaurant near the campus.

Seiji looks out the window. The clouds are hanging over the lake and a bank of darker clouds is just beyond. The snow seems to have let up. He watches Joan take a pair of socks from her pack, remove her own wet ones, and pull on the dry socks. Women's feet had always repelled Seiji. Joan's are doughy with short, bent toes. He could hardly wait for her to cover them again. Still, the act of changing her socks seems peculiarly domestic to Seiji, almost intimate. It reminds him of how his mother used to sweep her hand across the sheets to smooth out wrinkles as she laid out the bedding for the night. Joan's face is plain but when Seiji looks at her, he sees her with the candlelight on her face, bundled in her parka sitting cross legged on the sidewalk, holding her candle in both hands. He remembers Doug squatting in front of her, handing her a cup of tea he'd brought. She was looking at Doug and the light of her face seemed to emanate from inside, as though her face were a finely crafted lantern and her skin its translucent paper shade. Doug had looked at Joan lovingly, grateful for her participation in the vigil and concerned that she was sitting on the ground on such a cold evening. Admiration for Joan wells within Seiji just recalling the scene.

"Did you notice a place to have dinner? I'm getting hungry," Joan says, still massaging her cold feet.

"Yes, there were a couple of places where we got off the bus. One was right on the lake."

The cafe is homey and empty. They sit at a table next to windows where they can see the sun setting behind the mountains just beyond Lake Ashi. Seiji orders cuttlefish pizza and beer for them and by the time they finish, the snow has stopped although the sky is clouded over obscuring any stars. They don't say much, each feeling the other is content just to be in the company of the other, wrapped in the scenic Japanese mountains. After dinner, they walk along the side of the winding road, first Seiji and then Joan, back to their minshuku.

Once in the room, Joan feels awkward. The atmosphere for their love-making had always been accidental. It had always begun haphazardly, after a chilly vigil where comrades, faces still glowing warm from the candles they'd held, walked each other home offering each other a cheery o yasumi nasai at the door. Or, after earnest discussions with Doug in pubs where they'd perhaps turned over one too many sake decanters.

"This is almost like a honeymoon," Joan blushes, giggling uneasily. Unbuttoning her blouse, she immediately regrets the remark. Would Seiji think Joan meant that a night spent together like this was as good as a promise? The mention of a honeymoon was bound to be heard as a mention of marriage. Seiji, though, didn't seem to have heard. Joan isn't quite sure how much to take off. Would it be too bold to be completely naked? Should she leave on the pink satin bikini panties she wore? He might like to be the one to remove them. Or, would he rather she undress herself?

Seiji is silent. He's now very concerned by the fact that he doesn't want to kiss Joan. He feels a certain amount of pressure to manufacture at least the seeds of desire but he doesn't quite know how to go about it. He recalls Joan's face, not as she is this moment, slipping under the covers in only her panties, but with Doug squatting in front of her offering her tea; Doug lighting his candle from her flame. How soft she looked in that candlelight! And, Doug, how earnestly he knelt beside her! Doug was fond of Joan; there was no question. And Seiji was almost certain that Doug thought Joan and Seiji made a good pair.

Joan is suddenly thinking of Doug too. What a contrast Doug and Seiji made, standing on the sidewalk after walking her home. She would look back over her shoulder at them as she fiddled with her key. She watches Seiji pull off his jeans, sliding them down legs that are tense and light like a gymnast's and she thinks of Doug.

"Doug asked me to talk to Kathy Brooks about joining the group," says Joan as Seiji settles in beside her.

"Will you?"

"I told him he ought to ask her himself because he's really the strength of the group. Half the people are in the group because of Doug."

"Yes, he's quite the dynamo." Seiji rests his hand on Joan's bare waist.

"Hmmmm," says Joan. "If it weren't for him..." but her voice trails off.

"What? If it weren't for Doug what?" he says slipping his fingers inside Joan's satin panties.

Guam USA

The sun shifts leaving the back of Naomi's legs exposed to the full brutality of the Pacific sun. She stirs, wanting relief from the heat, worrying that her fair legs will burn...toys with the idea of moving her lounger, dragging it again under the drifting shade of the umbrella and wonders if perhaps a flick of her wrist will toss the beach towel over her legs. Her face sweats against the plastic slats of the lounger. The thick, hot air mutes the sound of the children playing just beyond her feet; it would be so easy to sink again into drowsy lethargy. Next to her on the table, a paper cup, lukewarm water, the remains of ice from a cola. Naomi stretches out her hand. Leaving her eyes closed, she gropes for the cup.

Bill left the beach for the pool an hour ago: submerged bar stools, a straw canopy of shade...Bill sipping a midori concoction with fruit garnish. Naomi wants to join him. Turning, she sits and blinks open her eyes, slides her sunglasses over her well-oiled nose, and pulls the last of the water through the straw. She gathers the few things she'd brought: a new American novel from the hotel shop, wristwatch, tanning lotion, postcards that are left unwritten. It's four p.m. The worst of the sun is gone.

Naomi moves from the glaring white sands of the beach, up the stairs through the orchids that spill over the terraced walls, into the shade of an umbrella at a poolside table where Bill left his camera and newspaper. The sun has made Naomi's head ache and her lips feel hot and cracked. Bill is in the water at the bar. He hasn't noticed that Naomi has come up, but he glances over at the table to make sure his camera is still there. When he sees her, he waves.

"Bring me a drink, will you," Naomi calls to Bill. The air seems almost too thick to carry sound. Calling out like that, her voice drifting across the pool over the half-dozen bobbing Japanese heads, seems such an American thing to do. It makes her feel big, aware of her American-sized breasts and thighs, and of her veined and freckled skin. Still, she doesn't have the energy to walk around the pool to order a drink herself.

"What?" Bill yells back, unselfconsciously.

"A drink. Get me a drink," she yells, even louder this time.

"I know that. What kind?"

"Doesn't matter. Something juicy." Not a single face looks toward their noise. Naomi sits down after this last effort, flinging her sunglasses on the table and rubbing her stinging eyes.

Bill has bought a *Los Angeles Times* from the hotel where they are staying. The front page shows a bombed out marketplace in Baghdad. The caption is "Multiple Explosions Rock Baghdad." The paper is three days old. They'd heard the story on CNN before they'd left Tokyo. Still, the paper is a treat. They're on vacation and, now, Bill has both an American paper *and* time to work the crossword puzzle.

In a few minutes Bill comes toward her balancing two drinks. A bag of peanuts is wedged between his elbow and body. It's their first relief in a year of living abroad—still, a picture of the American president in the airport and American dollars don't quite make Guam America.

"What's this?" She takes the glass he hands her, frothy and milky, topped with spears of pineapple and a maraschino cherry.

"Uh, Ta-ta I think it's called."

"What's in it?"

"The usual. Coconut milk and un…I don't know…some kind of liquor."

It really doesn't matter. It's cool and wet. Naomi's headache dissipates after a few sips. Above their table, a loud speaker plays something American.

"You know who this is?"

Bill cocks an ear. "I lost track of American music at least six months ago."

"Maybe Red Hot Chili Peppers?"

Bill shrugs.

Naomi props her feet on an empty chair and settles back. Bill sits across from her, folded newspaper resting on his paunchy stomach, pencil suspended over the crossword puzzle.

"This is nice," Naomi says, her words riding the wave of a deep exhale.

Bill grunts, glancing up as he pushes his half-moon glasses higher on his nose, then returns his attention to the puzzle. His chest is red from the sun except where the hair is thickest.

"Anything in the news?" she asks, ready for conversation.

"The usual," he mutters. He's agitated because she's interrupting his puzzle. "Ummm…Roman kitchen god?" His question is designed to draw her attention to his preoccupation, not to probe her deep well of trivia. He feigns remembering and writes it in.

In front of her, a slight Japanese man in European style swimsuit and a cowboy hat shows his companion the gun he's made of his hand. He demonstrates his shooting stance—how he'd stood facing the target, legs planted, spread just shoulder-width apart, both hands gripping the gun handle, arms taut, elbows locked—and, the kick of the Magnum or Lugar, or Colt or whatever, his arms flying up with the force, a grin spreading over his face, his listener amazed, amused.

Neon outlines of cowboys mounted high on boxy buildings line the route from the Guam airport to the Japanese hotels. The signs promise six shooters, cowgirls and ten-gallon hats. Japanese guns are for yakuza, Japanese mafia, but Guam is America and guns can be examined like a provocative book in a non-lending library, test driven like a new car, tried on like a pair of jeans.

At the shallow end of the pool, a young mother pulls a child in a Mickey Mouse float ring around the pool. Three men sit on the stools at the bar. A line of towel-covered girls sleep facing the fading sun, their loungers at the rail overlooking the ocean. Bill finishes the puzzle and tosses the paper aside. The loud speaker blares Madonna, one of the old tunes. He hums not knowing the words and, like Naomi, watches the would-be cowboy.

"This whole gun thing is a riot," Naomi says.

"Probably swings his invisible nine iron waiting on the train platform in the morning too. Imaginary props---part of his wardrobe." Bill gestures toward Naomi's book, closed on the table. "How is it?"

"Crap. Have you read any of this guy's stuff?" She picks up the book and shows him the cover but doesn't wait for his response. "I don't know. Maybe young people are like that these days. The characters are boring, they lead boring empty lives, they've accepted the fact that life is meaningless, so the book goes along not meaning anything. Didn't we, I mean our generation, force life to mean something, Bill? Didn't we at least try to make life mean something?"

"Nobody gets killed?"

"Well, people die of drug overdoses, fast cars, sexually transmitted diseases; they die of stupidity, boredom, and prosperity."

"Hmmm…should have bought the Clancy."

A new member joins the two men across the pool from Naomi and Bill. The man in the cowboy hat, the shooter, is again describing his prowess at the range. Each time he repeats, his new listener intent, the shooter thrusts his narrow hips forward slightly more, pushes his hat a little farther back. He adds a cigarette; it dangles from a loose lip, but the concentration on the target is the same each time.

"The Marlboro Man," Naomi chuckles.

"You want to go to the little place down the beach for dinner?" He shells a peanut and tosses it up to his mouth, reaches across the table to grab Naomi's drink and sucks noisily, pulling the foam through the straw. After a late breakfast, they'd skipped lunch.

"You mean that crummy little plywood dive with graffiti all over it? The one on the public beach?"

"Ahh, yes. The dreaded public beach. Beware the public beach," Bill says going into his B-movie previews voice, "American servicemen hauling insidious coolers, Frisbees, and radios in quantity enough to stock a convenience store. Volley ball nets, guitars, beach blankets, lawn chairs, charcoal grills in mind-boggling array. Watch while the Japanese, who never openly gawk, steal sideways glances. Watch while the scrawny, hairless Japanese man, trailed by his equally slight and hair-denuded Japanese wife, buy beers one at a time from the concession at the edge of the hotel's private beach, careful to deposit the empty cup in the battered Love-Your-Beach receptacle! The huge, hairy American sailors, on the other hand, haul six packs from massive coolers and toss cans of cold brewsky out to buddies submerged in the warm Pacific water up to their lips, all the while yelling for them to keep their fuckin' heads up, here comes a flyer." Bill returns to his normal, salesman's voice. "Yes, Naomi, that's the one I mean."

"You can't be serious," she says knowing perfectly well he is. "Even those she-sailors or she-tars or whatever it is you call them behave outrageously. I can't imagine what fun you think that is."

"My very favorite outrageous behavior…young, long-legged, blonde she-sailors whose beach garb is so slight as to appear absent from a near distance. Makes my palms sweat just thinking about them. The wavy-Navy. Crass, over-sized Americans yelling at each other when one blatantly encroaches on the other's staked-out space; they spread out their beach towels as if every place were Texas. Tsk, tsk. By dinner, the whole bunch of them will be barfin'-blind drunk. But that dive, as you call it, Naomi dear, has barbequed chicken wings, icey cold American beer and potato skins, greasy and crunchy."

"Five hundred drunken sailors barfing on my chicken wings…I don't think so. Why don't we just eat a nice salad in the hotel?"

But Bill's mind is set on some lively, if passive, entertainment. He wants at least to watch other people have fun even if he doesn't have any himself. Besides, a closer look at a Navy girl wearing one of those suits that expose the entirety of her bare buttocks, butt-floss or butt-thong or something, would absolutely make his day. Still, if Naomi's going to mope, it wouldn't be any fun.

"Go if you want," she tells Bill. "It wouldn't be the first time I've eaten alone. It's just I'm rather enjoying this peace and quiet. This is nice after a year in Tokyo." Bill looks sheepish and wonders if, later, she'll resent his leaving her alone. "Go. Honestly, I don't mind. You've paid your dues in sushi, sake, and boring business meetings. You deserve to get a closer look at some of these briney she-buns."

She can almost see the saliva dripping from the corner of his mouth. Beer, a plate of chicken wings, and a semi-clad female body is almost as good as being back in Santa Monica.

"I'll just go for a snack. Then we can have dinner around seven. How's that?" He suspects he may be lying but he isn't sure yet.

"Fine. I won't wait if you're late." Naomi hides herself behind her novel. She suspects he's at the very least misjudging himself. Once he gets caught up in the Americans (they're bound to have a pool table in there or darts or pinball), he won't be back for a while.

Bill changes from his reading glasses to his sunglasses. He buttons his shirt only at the waist and runs his fingers through his sparse hair.

"Be back in a jiffy."

"No need to hurry."

Naomi watches him walk away. The bulk of his body and his ruddy skin mark him as a tourist in his own country.

Bill disappears down the orchid path. Naomi reads; the story barely holds her attention. She looks up frequently, sucking sporadically at the empty Ta-ta. Maybe an hour or more passes. The girls at the rail stir, pack up their bags, and head inside the hotel. A Japanese man climbs out of the pool, dries his hands and lights a Marlboro.

Across the pool, a group looking suspiciously like sailors spill noisily up the stairs from the public beach, five of them, three men and two women. The blonde woman wears a bikini; the brunette covers hers with a t-shirt. Immediately, the heaviest male of the three breaks away from the group, and giving a war hoop, cannonballs into the pool. A second male follows suit as the other three slip quietly down into the pool and swim for the bar stools. The two canonballers begin to pass a football from one end of the pool to the other. The heavy one rattles a stream of football-play commentary. "He goes deep, running like hell, he's at the thirty…" His voice is husky, the kind toughened by cigarettes and hard drinking. He pulls his arm way back and lets the ball fly. It lands flat, uncaught. Waves ripple the pool. The young Japanese mother turns her head to avoid the splash; she and her daughter drift over to the side of the pool and climb out. Then, the heavy one plants a pass ball in the middle of the blonde woman's back. Her head snaps back and her drink sloshes. Angry, she turns.

"Hey, asshole, watch it? I'm drinkin' here," she screams, keeping an eye on her drink and letting the ball float in front of her.

"Sorreee, Sherreee," he taunts. "Rich is the asshole. He was supposed to catch the fuckin' ball." He paddles his way through the water toward her. "Besides, I haven't drowned you in an hour or so." He grabs her by the neck and dowses her. Sherry comes up laughing, sputtering, swinging with one hand, holding her drink high and level with the other. Rich grabs the ball and the play begins again. Sherry downs her drink and joins them.

This is exactly what Naomi wanted to avoid—this kind of drunken horseplay. It always ended with men fighting, somebody exposing himself to piss in the pool or someone throwing chairs through windows. No group of sailors this drunk ever walked away humming with their hands in their pockets. Still, she wasn't going to let this group of rowdies drive her away when the sun was just about to set over the ocean. Naomi slides down in her chair and, resting her head on the chair back, turns the page.

This time the ball strays into the group of three Japanese men. The ball hits squarely against the chest of a man who is thrown back by the impact of it. Stunned, he lets the ball wallow in his lap.

The cannonballer, the heavy one, not Rich, climbs out of the pool. "Sorry, man. You okay? You understand English?" He retrieves the football from the Japanese man's lap and tosses it from one hand to the other. Then, turning to the guy in the cowboy hat, "Hey, didn't I see you at the range? Look, Rich, it's Lucky Three Fingers!" The Americans had given him that name because he was a deadly shot even though he used three fingers to pull the trigger. "Hell of a shot! Taddeo? Am I right?" He is right. They'd talked at the shooting range. Taddeo is pleased to have confirmation of his abilities at the range. They shake hands. Addressing Taddeo's friends, he says, "This guy's and ace shooter, d'you know that? An ACE!"

Taddeo, speaking to his companions in Japanese, explains where he'd met this massive, too white guy in jams almost to his knees.

"You guys want to toss the ball around?"

Again, Taddeo speaks to his friends. Naomi isn't sure if none of the Japanese understand the question or whether they are conferring—getting consensus—on whether they want to "toss the ball around." After some discussion, Taddeo thanks him but declines.

"Suit yourself," the American calls back over his shoulder, already jumping back down into the pool.

Naomi shuts her book, turns her attention to the sun sinking lower over the water. The noise of the play distracts her, destroys her concentration. The Americans shout a drink order to the bartender. The woman and her little girl have gone leaving only Naomi, the three Japanese men, and the five Americans. Again, the ball flies into Taddeo's group, this time hitting Taddeo on the side of the head and knocking off his cowboy hat. The American approaches, pretends embarrassment, apologizes, sets Taddeo's hat in place and waits for the return of the ball that Taddeo has picked up.

"Sure you don't want to play?" the heavy one asks. No discussion this time; they don't want to play. Taddeo lobs the ball back.

"Come on, Taddeo, Buddy! What the hell? You call that a pass?" Taddeo laughs uncomfortably, sinking back into the lounger.

The Americans huddle. They break and head for Taddeo's little group. "Come on, Taddeo, let me show you how to throw a pass. We'll turn you into a real Dallas Cowboy!" The football team, now all five of the Americans have joined in, lifts Taddeo by his arms and legs and throws him in the pool. Taddeo's a sport. He seems willing to play along. The other Japanese man laughs heartily but the late comer slowly walks away, down the stairs to the beach.

Naomi makes a wide path around the pool to avoid being splashed, heading toward the bar on her way to another Ta-ta. The sun and drinking on an empty stomach have made her a little light-headed. Still, another drink sounds good. At the bar, a hotel security guard, a Chamorro, stands talking to the bartender. His dark blue uniform smacks of police garb. The stripes on his sleeve and the wings over his shirt pocket are designed to intimidate. His name badge is kroy-typed. Naomi feels for him. Obviously, the bartender called the guard to shoo the pesky trespassers away from the paying guests. The guard is half the size of any one of the Americans and his eyes are darting between the commotion in the pool and the bartender. The guard's hand rests nervously on the leather cover that straps down his service revolver.

Naomi wants to order a drink but she feels awkward. She doesn't want to interrupt. The hotel guard's most dangerous assignment, no doubt, is to escort the night's receipts to the Brinks truck and now he's faced with five drunken sailors, at least two of whom he can expect to be belligerent. She waits for a break in the conversation. Suddenly, the ball comes skidding across the bar, crashing into the pyramid of wineglasses sending them flying. Naomi ducks involuntarily. The tile floor is instantly showered with glistening crystalline shards. Broken fragments scoot across the floor and hit the wall behind her. The ringleader, the heavy-set sailor, swims over to retrieve the ball and realizes that the ball has come to its final resting place smack at the feet of the hotel guard.

"You folks registered guests?" The guard's accent is slight, the island-flavored English spoken in Guam.

Naomi tenses. The quiver in the guard's voice blows his credibility right up front.

"Sure. We're guests, ain't we?" The heavy one is out of the pool, a good head taller than the guard and twice as wide. The sailor's suit drips water onto the guard's shoes. He looks back over his shoulder at his team. Rich looks defiant, his chin pushed out and his hands on his hips. The others hesitate, ready to turn and run back down the stairs, safely back to the public beach.

"Can I see your room keys, please sir?"

"Keys? Uh…we left our keys in our rooms. Yup…stupid, huh? We're all locked out."

The guard picks up the bar phone. "What's your name and room number? I'll need to confirm." His voice has picked up confidence but Naomi sees that the guard's hand is trembling.

"Hey, man, you don't believe us? Hey, guys, this officer here doesn't believe us."

"I'll have to ask you to leave unless I can confirm that you're registered guests, sir." The guard and the bartender keep a steady eye on the sailor. The sailor stares directly back at the guard, facing him down.

"I think the officer's gotten a little over heated, don't you, Rich. Must've been in the sun too long. Ain't that right, you guys? The big tough officer must have sun stroke or something." He takes a step forward as he speaks. "Don't you think he's a little too hot, Rich? We ought to cool this guy off. This guy needs a good soak."

The dark woman, not Sherry, touches his arm. "Let's go, Tim. It's getting late."

"I'll go when I'm fuckin' good and ready to go, sweetheart. You think this little twit Chamorro is gonna run me off?"

"Come on, Tim. Don't be a dick." She tugs his arm.

Naomi is afraid to move. Glass litters the floor in front of the bar and her feet are bare. The sun is getting fainter but the nightlights haven't yet come on.

"Tim, buddy, let's go." It's the third male, the one closest to sober.

"I told you, I'll go when I go and not before. This guy is getting on my nerves. I think we ought to throw the little greaser in the pool. You with me, Rich?"

"Sure." Rich's speech is slurred. He couldn't have much strength; even his legs look a little rubbery.

The security guard begins to back away. Naomi doesn't really see him pull his pistol, but she realizes that the noise she hears is the sound of the holster snapping open. Seconds later, she sees the outline of his gun against the sunset, a black silhouette against a red sky like a televised scene from a Dashiel Hammet novel. Tim and Rich jump him and wrestle him toward the pool, all the while laughing and carrying on, not knowing themselves that the guard has drawn his gun. Taddeo, who'd hung back looking stricken, has crossed the pool and is climbing out when the gun goes off, a wild shot, an accident or a shot intended to scare. Taddeo staggers, falls into the pool, his blood spreading through the water. Everyone stops. The guard is paralyzed.

Before Naomi knows it, the Americans have disappeared down the steps, leaving behind only a bloodstained foot print where one of them had cut a foot.

The bartender calls the front desk. He's frantic, asking them to get the police and an ambulance. The guard fishes Taddeo out of the pool. No one else moves. Pretty soon Naomi hears the sirens.

Everything is surreal. Time moves in some kind of dense haze. Someone brings a chair so Naomi can sit down. Bill appears. Police had run down the beach just ahead of him. It's dark now and the pool lights cast a harsh white glare on Naomi and on the policeman standing over her taking notes. The starkness of the lights smack of old-fashioned interrogation: the policeman's foot propped on Naomi's chair, using his knee to support his notepad, not looking at her but only at his pen moving across his paper.

Naomi remembers the names, Tim, the heavy-set one; Rich, taller, leaner, and darker than Tim; Sherry, the blonde. She didn't remember hearing the names of the other two.

Bill waits impatiently for the policeman to finish. He shifts on his feet, looking around trying to piece together what's happened, twisting the sunglasses he holds in his hands. A hotel attendant sweeps up glass around the bar. Another policeman questions the bartender. Someone strings yellow police tape across the door preventing anyone from entering the pool area. A siren starts up again, then fades as it moves away.

Still writing, the policeman backs away from Naomi. She stands and walks over to Bill.

"What happened?"

Naomi hesitates. "Someone got shot," she tells him.

"Are you okay? Who got shot?" He looks her over searching for some small wound.

Bill puts his arm around Naomi's waist, supporting her. Her face is red with the sun; soft, white flesh rings her eyes where they have been protected by her sunglasses. Her hair is blown stiff, away from her face.

Bill reeks of beer. Barbeque sauce lingers in the corner of his mouth and dots his shirt with bright red spots.

"Who got shot?" Bill asks again looking searchingly into Naomi's face.

"That cowboy," she mutters almost inaudibly.

Naomi takes a long shower that night. Bill orders a club sandwich from room service for her. An old black and white movie flickers on TV, the sound a murmur, while she nibbles at her sandwich.

"They should be guilty of something more than trespassing or malicious mischief," Naomi shakes her head indignantly. "It doesn't seem right."

"But the sailors didn't have a gun, Naomi. From your account, they may not have even known that the guard had a gun, much less that he'd drawn it."

"Still." She is frustrated and Bill knows she'll think of nothing else for days. "They provoked the whole thing. I mean it never would have happened if they hadn't been where they didn't belong. Isn't there some kind of…I don't know…manslaughter. Something?"

Bill shrugs. He sells auto parts to Japanese dealers of American cars. He doesn't know beans about provocation. He takes the pickle off her plate and eats it.

"They never should have been there in the first place," she says. "They were drunk. They had no business there."

"Nothing's going to happen to the guard, Naomi. I doubt he'll even lose his job. It was an accident. The guy who got shot? He'll be fine. He'll have a great story to tell."

"Bill, it's not a case of all's well that ends well. Those American sailors are responsible for what happened!"

"The guy with the gun is responsible, Naomi."

"He's a guard! He's supposed to have a gun!" Naomi is defensive, angry. Then, quietly, "He just fell back in the water, Bill. I thought it was a joke at first. I thought he was just fooling around."

Bill stretches out on the bed and turns up the volume on the TV. In five minutes, he is sound asleep. Naomi toys with her sandwich, watches the commercials flash garish color around the dark room and thinks about her postcards.

The Ballad of Rhonda Ise

Two kinds of bars exist on that straight and treeless stretch of Highway 64 between Stringtown and Poplar Bluff; the basic Holiday Inn-neutral carpet-indirect lighting-mood music bar mainly referred to as a lounge, and the other kind, the concrete-floor, wooden-walled shit-kicker bars. Shit-kicker bars were off the main square of the old town, not out on the highway that town people still referred to as new; they were one-story, long, low sheds with gravel parking lots and dark, smoky back rooms where the country bands played. Walking into The Moose Lodge seemed like walking into a time capsule where my life was preserved and, after two years away, I'm not sure whether my aim is to resuscitate that life or to bury it once and for all. Every secret I ever had is in The Moose in somebody's memory besides my own. I spot Suzie Hyde right away, sitting where she sat the last time I was here, at a table littered with empty glasses and beer bottles, tapping her cigarette ashes into a wrinkled aluminum foil ashtray.

"How you been, Sooz?" I yell above the lilt and twang of the country music.

"Rhonda! Where you been, girl?" Her face lights up, she stands, and gives me a hug. "I ain't seen you since, hell, I don't know. A long time."

I left Stringtown two days after high school graduation more than twenty years ago. I left, I suppose, because if I'd stayed, I'd always be the poor girl from the run-down house by the railroad tracks. Still, here I am again, living my Stringtown life in my favorite bar, not only ready but looking forward to listening to the Stringtown boys' bullshit. As they say, you can take the girl out of the country…. This time I'd stayed away two years. I'd never stayed away that long. I breathe in The Moose like it's my mother's pot roast; nothing has ever brought a smile to my face like the smell of The Moose on a Saturday night; it's like stepping inside a beer keg. Not much changes: all the men still smell of Old Spice and spearmint gum. No man in a lounge ever smelled like a Stringtown boy in The Moose.

"You look like a lady could use a Screaming Orgasm," Eddie Welton's broad face is tanned below his eyes where the shade from the brim of his sunhat stops. His hair is permanently crimped from the hat band. He grins at me.

"Oh, for god's sake, Rhonda, it's a drink. Take the bastard up on it," Suzie urges still tapping the ashes from her cigarette and not looking up. "It's the best offer you'll get all night. It's better than last week. The drink of the week was an Enema. Can you believe that? Poor Lynette had to go around asking everybody how they'd like a nice cold Enema." Suzie chuckled in spite of herself.

"I can hardly wait 'til the drink of the week is a Blow Job," Eddie's boyish face shines. "Sweet little Lynette can offer me a Blow Job anytime. In fact, I'd take two."

"You're a helluva man, Eddie," Suzie says.

I had known Suzie and Eddie since the days when we all used to catch fireflies in Suzie's front yard. Then, we got old enough to kick up dust speeding through the cornfields in Eddie's '55 Ford.

"One Screaming Orgasm for the lady," Eddie yells to Lynette.

The table fills up. Martha and Ray sit down, order a couple of beers, then get up to dance. The band is playing a Texas Two Step. Suzie tells me Arleen is pregnant and that Ray lost his job at the sawmill in Elsinore. It's the news. But, it sounds like the same damn news I hear every time I come to Stringtown. Nothing really changes. Johnny either. It's almost midnight before I feel his hands on my shoulders as he bends down to whisper in my ear, "When's the last time you had a Screaming Orgasm?"

"About a half hour ago, Johnny. You're a little late."

"Well, in that case, let's dance."

I take his hand and follow him to the dance floor. Johnny is tall and lean. His black hair, already beginning to grey, hangs down on his collar in curls. It's a slow tune and Johnny holds me tight and close. His soft worn shirt brushes against my cheek as we dance; his snakeskin cowboy boots means he's dressed for a serious Saturday night.

"I heard somebody on the radio the other day saying that our generation'll use the day John Kennedy got shot as the milestone in their lives. That everybody will remember what they were doing on that day their whole lives like the generation before us remembers Pearl Harbor." Johnny's mouth is pressed against my ear. His breath is warm. The smell of spearmint goes straight down my spine.

"I would have remembered anyway, Johnny," I almost coo.

November 22, 1963. That day, Johnny caught up with me as I walked to school, cruising slowly beside me, his elbow hanging out the window of his Chevy as he gave me a pitch about spending the day with him at the lake house instead of going to school. He stretched out his hand to touch my skirt with his fingertips. I'd gotten in the car beside him feeling like we were Bonnie and Clyde about to rob a bank.

I remember Johnny's beat-up cowboy boot pressing the gas pedal in jerky bursts making the Chevy lurch forward, and then roll smoothly until it reached the next muddy hole in the dirt ruts that passed for a road to Red Angel Lake and to the Reynolds's cabin. In late November, the leafless twigs struck out against the windshield and, on this day, the sun was bright with high, white clouds. Soon the road curved and cleared and the silent cabin, almost invisible against the black rise of the ridge, appeared. I'd be lying if I said my whole insides didn't clutch; I could barely breathe because I knew already what was going to happen. It made me feel sick but not a bad sick; it was a sick like being first in line for a roller coaster ride—fear and hesitation mixed with complete commitment.

If it had been summer, even at this early morning hour, voices would have been heard across the lake from the occasional boaters out for a morning paddle. In those days, the Reynolds cabin was the only one on the lake. It was quiet and deserted and Johnny and I would lie down in the grass on a summer's night and he would swear he could hear the stars move.

Somewhere in my head it registered that I just missed English class and I should be on my way to history. Instead, Johnny held my hand leading me to the cabin, unlocking the door, and ushering me inside. It was cold and I thought it looked like snow might fall from those white clouds, but Johnny didn't want to build a fire. Instead, he said, "Why don't we get under the covers?"

We were completely dressed when we laid ourselves down but I knew Johnny already had an erection and that terrified me. Still, we moved forward like lemmings going over a cliff.

This is what, among other things, we couldn't have known: the amount of blood my virgin damn had in its reservoir. Johnny's parents' bed looked like Johnny had butchered me, dismembered me. I don't know why I felt embarrassed, apologetic. Johnny had seen blood before, shot and dressed a deer, but now, as he felt the warmth of my blood against his naked body, he jumped up and threw the covers back as though something terrible and unforeseen had happened.

"Get up!" he yelled at me. "Quick! Come on! Get off the bed!"

Honestly, at that point I couldn't speak, much less move. I was lying in a pool of my own blood. Johnny loosed the sheets from the mattress and wrapped them around me and carried me into the bathroom where he dumped the bloody sheets and me into the bathtub. He went back into the bedroom, I guess to check on the condition of the mattress, paced from the bathroom to the bedroom a few times before he knelt beside me wrapped in a bloody sheet sitting in his bathtub. I'd never seen a naked man before but here was Johnny, private parts and his thighs red with my blood. He turned on the water in the sink, grabbed a wash cloth, and began to scrub the blood away. I sat dumb-founded, not moving, just watching like some idiot child who had done something wrong.

When Johnny was dressed again, he came into the bathroom with a space heater, and turning it on, said, "Why don't you clean yourself up? I'll get your clothes and make us some tea. I think that's all there is."

We sat on his couch looking out at the lake, playing some new 45s that he bought, "I'm leaving it all up to you," and "Since I fell for you," me getting up every so often to swap out one wash cloth for another, keeping the bloody sheet and wash cloths in the bathtub of hot water and bleach. I thought surely the blood would stop but when the last school bell rang and it was time for me to go home, I was still bleeding.

Johnny covered the seat of his truck with shop rags just in case and we drove home silently. I had planned to walk into my house and directly into my the bathroom where I could replace the washcloth with a sanitary napkin and tell my mother I'd started my period unexpectedly, but when I got inside my mother's red eyes made me sure the school had called home and that my mother knew every detail of what happened that day down to the wash cloth I'd folded to catch my virgin blood. But I was wrong; instead, President Kennedy had been shot and the loss of my virginity seemed confused with a whole different scale of things. There was something mystical about the shedding of my own blood on that day, as though it was the same blood that stained Jacqueline Kennedy's pink suit, as though my blood knew hers, a bond that practically made us sisters. It was like a secret shared between the First Lady in the pink pillbox hat and this little nobody from Stringtown. Mom had been amazed when I told her I hadn't heard about it in school.

Mom and I sat in front of the television, confused and weeping, watching Walter Cronkite as this terrible thing unfolded, as Lyndon Johnson was sworn in and Jackie Kennedy stared vacantly.

Now, back at The Moose, back in Johnny's arms, the band started playing a twanging version of "Since I fell for you." I guess it was still our song even twenty years later. After The Moose Lodge closed, everyone fell into Turner's All-Nite Truck Stop as if we'd been tilted off a giant game board depositing all of us into spots around red Formica tables. I sat down in the booth across from Eddie and Suzie while Johnny used the men's room.

"He's got a girlfriend, ya know." This isn't news. Suzie's face is in her menu but her glazed eyes are on me.

"So? He's always gone out. We're not married, Suzie. Hell, we aren't even dating. I haven't seen the man in two years!" I go back to my menu. Too many Screaming Orgasms have turned my brain to mush.

"This is different," Suzie says.

"You're a bitch, you know that Suzie?" Eddie glares at her.

"Shut up, Eddie! Rhonda," here Suzie pauses for effect. "Johnny's dating a high school cheerleader. Eighteen! She says they're engaged."

Johnny slides in beside me and looks around the table. "Whatsa matter?"

Nobody says anything but the way he looks at Suzie and Eddie tells him what he doesn't want to ask.

Later, ketchup in the corners of his mouth, Johnny turns to me, "I know what," he says, "Let's go out to the lake house like old times. Want to, Rhonnie? We ain't been there for years. We can play old records. How'd that be?"

I am thirty-eight and haven't had a date in six years. That's all I could think about as we drove the familiar territory to Red Angel Lake. The road was paved sometime in the seventies and a few restaurants now dotted what is officially Red Angel Ridge Road. There are new homes and not just scattered vacation homes either, but whole subdivisions. With all the changes, though, the Reynolds cabin looks pretty much the same. Inside the cabin, the puzzles and card games are still on the bookcase shelf and the fishing rods are still in the corner. The floor has been replaced and, outside, a tin canopy has been built to shelter a speedboat. The moon is bright and I can tell that a sidewalk now runs along the lakeside. Some benches and trash cans are at the water's edge.

Unlike 1963, this is a warmish November weekend after a bitter week of snow but it is still cold enough that inside the cabin Johnny and I can see our breath.

"It's cold in here!" Johnny rubs his arms and then mine. "Let's get under the covers."

"You got to be kidding, right?"

"What?"

He shrugs and stuffs some newspapers and kindling into the cast iron stove. "You want a shot to warm you up?"

"Tea?"

"I can do tea." I hear him rattling around the kitchen, then the water splashing into the pan. Cabinets bang as Johnny searches for the tea. The kindling catches and the room begins to warm. Johnny hands me a cup and sits down on the couch with his whiskey.

"Com'on over here and sit by me." Johnny pats the couch next to him.

I stand next to the stove. The fire is warm on my face now so I unzip my parka and let the warmth spread to my chest. "When did you plan to tell me, Johnny?"

There is nothing to stop him from telling me to go to hell or that it's none of my damn business. Instead, he sets his whiskey down, takes off his jacket, and says, "She's so young, Rhonda." He sounds almost apologetic as though he's been caught in a trap young girls set for middle-aged men like him. "I'm forty years old and she's eighteen. I couldn't just seduce her and then throw her to the wolves."

What am I supposed to say? He doesn't owe me anything, certainly not his undying love. But somehow, that November day twenty years ago, stopped us, put up a roadblock neither of us were able to get completely past. What came out was, "I was younger than that. I was sixteen years old when I sat in a bloody mess in that bathtub. Remember?"

"Not the same. I was eighteen when you were sixteen. We were kids. We didn't know any better."

"And you do now?"

"Hell, doesn't look like it, does it." All the years of sun and hard work cast a net of fine lines on his tired face. Still, his grin kills me. There is only the light of the fire and the moonlight coming through the half-curtained window, but it made Johnny look….I don't know…rugged? Boyish?

"She's so pretty with her eighteen-year-old titties and her flat stomach, her long blond hair and smooth legs."

"Spare me the details. I'm supposed to feel sorry for you because you couldn't resist fucking somebody young enough to be your daughter. You're such an ass, Johnny!"

"Don't get mean, Rhonda. I'm torn up about this. You can see I am."

"Get up," I give his foot a kick, "I want to go home."

"Awww, don't be like that, Rhonnie. Take off your coat and stay with me awhile. We haven't been here in such a long time. It's great to see you, girl. You look great!"

I zip my parka and set down my cup. "Com'on old man. Time to take me home."

"Tracy's a mistake I can't take back. I knew the minute I saw those little cheerleader panties hit the floor I was doomed."

"Yeah, but what a way to go, right?"

"I couldn't stop. I didn't want to stop. And she wanted me too. That sweet little blonde high school girl wanted me too."

"Get over yourself." I almost whisper it because Johnny has gotten up and is standing close and his hand is making its way up inside my sweater.

"Have pity, Rhonnie. I'm a foolish old man who does foolish things."

"Yes, and you're doing something foolish right now." I take his hand from under my sweater but I know that's a gate that can't be shut again.

"You're the only one I've ever loved. You know that, don't ya Rhonnie?" And he is close again and I can smell spearmint and feel hot breath in my ear.

It is more that I want to make love to Johnny than that he wants to make love to me; at first I feel as though I'm reclaiming my territory but then I realize it's more like saying goodbye—not just to Johnny, but to Stringtown too: to everything I was before I moved to the city. The mattress was replaced no doubt long ago but the brass bed is the same. The moonlight comes in the window and across Johnny's bare back.

I look at Johnny now, sound asleep and snoring and I cover his naked body. I dress and take the car keys from the table beside the door where he left them and drive myself back to The Moose's now empty parking lot where I left my car.

Driving home I find myself wondering whether John Kennedy deserved the love that Jackie gave him. He was famous, smart, rich, handsome, and charming, but I know for damn sure that Johnny Reynolds didn't deserve the love I gave him and yet I couldn't stop loving him. I can't.

Still, the dark night and the empty highway, comfort me. I'm restoring the distance between Stringtown and me, each mile I breathe a little easier, relax back into my seat a little more. And, I know that every time John Kennedy is mentioned, every time Jackie O. is on a magazine cover, every time John Jr. or Caroline are mentioned, I'll think about Johnny Reynolds. The memories of Johnny and me on November 22, 1963 are sweet in a way but the day will be bitter always. Every anniversary of President Kennedy's death will be on the news the rest of my life and the torch will never be passed.

This is my Father's Coat

I am shot three times. The bullets go into me like sharp, hard fingers making their point. There is never oozing blood just three bullet holes like scarlet tacks that nail my silk blouse to my midriff. I stagger into the bedroom where Win sits on the bed tying the laces of his running shoes.

"Help me," I say breathlessly. "I've been shot."

"Can it wait?" he doesn't look up. He isn't irritated, just seeking information. "I'm just about to go for a run." He finishes tying his shoes and stands up.

I think perhaps he hasn't heard me correctly.

"I've been shot, Winston!"

"Suzanne, this will only take me two minutes." He pats my shoulder on his way out. "I'll be right back. Lots of people get shot, Coo. It'll be all right."

But, I know I won't be alive when he gets back. I know I won't last. I will have to walk to the hospital on my own. As I walk, I get weaker, bending over my wounds. With each step I look more frightful, more ghostly. I pass a couple on the street. I stagger toward them. "Help me," I plead, but they seem terrified of me and hurry away. I fall to the ground. Then, I see my father coming toward me. His dark blue overcoat is draped over his arm. When he reaches me, he doesn't seem to recognize me, but his face is tender, sad for this stranger lying wounded on the sidewalk. My father unfolds his coat and gently lays it over me, then walks away.

I've always been fond of sleep…the pleasure of it. There is pleasure in recurring dreams like this one, too. Oh, admittedly disturbing, but my heart thrills when Win calls me Coo. My heart throbs at my father's gentle gesture. There 's no such thing as a bad dream.

And, I love the anticipation of sleep, the feel of my bed especially in winter…sliding under my down comforter and feeling my shivers slowly dissipate. I look forward to the night's dream and how it will feel to wake from it. I know at the end of each day that I get to go to that alternate universe where I am queen.

This morning, I smile when I wake up, stretching and turning my head to look out the window at the sky. I probably woke because I heard the door close behind Win as he left for his Saturday morning jog. I breathe in the coffee he made for me before he left --brewed the coffee and set my favorite cup beside the coffeemaker, the big yellow cup with a brown crack the inside length of it, a crack like an intimate secret.

I like my cup and I like the steadiness of my life, the reliability of it. Win will be gone an hour, come in sweaty, head immediately to the immense fridge he'd insisted on buying, and tap his glass on the lever that will deliver first ice and then water. When he comes in, I will be leaning against the kitchen counter dressed in casual Saturday go-to-lunch clothes, my cup drawn close to my mouth but not drinking. We won't speak until he's downed a glass of water and begun pouring another. Then, I will say, "Did you have a good run?"

Win will answer as he always does, "It was okay," and then he'll set his glass in the sink, wipe his sweaty forehead with his arm, and leave me to take his shower.

That's how Saturdays go.

This Saturday, after my first cup of coffee, I take my shower and dress, pour a second cup of coffee, and lean against the kitchen counter to wait for Win. I stand there watching the minutes change on the stove's digital clock. Win, who is never late, is late. Half an hour goes by before I decide to sit down at the table and thumb through a four-month old *Woman's Day* that I had been keeping for the Key Lime Pie recipe. I'm not afraid. I know that Win will return saying that he'd decided to sit in the coffee shop or that he stopped in the park to watch the kids play soccer. He will say that he needed to think. I'll ask what about and he'll say, nothing special, Coo, just think.

Win still hasn't come home by the time I am ready to leave to meet my sister for lunch. I leave a note on the fridge right above the water dispenser. "Lunch with Ellen. See you around 2."

Oh my God...Ellen. Half the time I dread spending even an afternoon with her. Today is sort of like that. After our father had gone, Ellen and I were as close as eyes on a face, but that was a long time ago.

"You're not worried?" Ellen asks as we follow the hostess through the maze of tables to the one destined for us.

"He's had something on his mind lately." I shrug and shake my head slowly as we take our seats. The hostess walks back to her post without saying anything.

"Something? Like what?"

"I don't know," I say already impatient. Ellen can be so annoying.

"Well, is it work? Or money? Are you guys okay?" I don't answer. "He's not having an affair is he? How do you know he hasn't had an accident?"

I look at the menu while Ellen looks at me. I say, "If he'd had an accident, I would have heard. He always carries his cell with my number as the ICE."

"ICE?"

"In case of emergency. Someone would have called."

"But, what if he was hit and his phone was smashed, and…"

"Shut up, Ellen," I don't move my eyes from the menu. "Let's talk about something else."

Sometimes, I dream of Ellen. Ellen is two years younger than I am but somehow we seem almost like twins—I never take on the role of the protective older sister and Ellen rejects the role of the less powerful younger sister. Both of us seem equally powerless, equally unprotected. When I was twelve and Ellen was ten, our father went out for a pack of cigarettes and never came home. Another woman, no doubt, but he was too cowardly to tell us and so just walked out the door lighting the last cigarette in his pack. The last thing I remember about him is the sound of his fingers jingling the change in his pocket as the door closed behind him. Ellen and I never talk about it but once my mother told me that our father was a child molester and had left home to spare us. She'd said that he'd probably killed himself by now. I never told Ellen because I didn't believe my mother. She just told me that to make me feel that our father left because he loved us enough to protect us and not because he didn't. In what universe, I wondered, was it better to be a child molester than a man who had abandoned his wife and children? I could never dream about my mother. For years after, I expected to run into him at a filling station or some place and he wouldn't recognize me because I was older, but I would recognize him. Maybe I wouldn't even speak to him, just let him fill his tank and drive away while I watched him go one more time.

In my dream, Ellen and I share a small cage in a pet shop, like puppies from the same litter. It is silent except I can hear birds chirping. She and I are sitting alertly but not fearfully, looking out of our cage at whoever walks through the door. Then our father walks in and is standing by our cage. He bends over and sticks his finger through the cage to scratch my head. I don't know if he recognizes us. He doesn't seem to; he just stares at us for a while before asking the pet shop attendant how much for a canary. I watch him walk away in his dark blue coat.

"You didn't answer my question, Suzanne. Do you think he's having an affair?"

"You know, Ellen, I don't have a clue. My guess would be no. He seems into his job, seems to be looking forward to finishing his doctorate. We don't fight about money. " I had said all I intended to say. "Now, let's change the subject."

The server is a perky, young girl. It always seemed to me as if waitresses are either too perky or too sullen. I don't know which is worse. I still hadn't decided what to order and, in fact, I am thinking that I need to go home and lean against the kitchen counter with my yellow cup until Win walks through the door and pours his glass of water. But, I can't move; I sit there across from Ellen staring down into my menu.

I said that the pet shop dream is about Ellen and that's how I think of it. I have another dream of my father, my father in that dark blue coat, or rather it's a dream about my father's coat.

In the dream, I am looking for my father. My dreams are usually sparsely set, a big, bare room with a brown floor and brown walls. I look for my father in this room where he couldn't possibly hide; there are no chairs, no closets, no desks—if he were here I'd see him at once. Nonetheless, I call him, "Daddy? Are you here? Where are you?" And of course there's nothing there but the hollow ring of my own voice. Then, I notice in the corner of the room, in a shadow, a coat rack. On the coat rack, there is a navy blue overcoat and I go take a closer look. I take the coat off the rack and hold it up. I say, "Yes, this is my father's coat."

"I'll have chicken salad on whole wheat toast," I finally tell the perky waitress.

"My God, Suzanne, you always order that!"

"I like chicken salad."

"Something to drink?" asks the perky waitress.

"Just water, thanks." When the waitress takes away the menus, there is no barrier between me and Ellen. "And what's up with you?" I ask her.

"Oh, still seeing Dave," she says as if she were saying, oh, my hemorrhoids aren't as bad as they used to be.

It is hard for me to read Ellen's expression exactly. Is it disappointment? Boredom? Perhaps disappointment mixed with relief that he's still there? Ellen had already been married and divorced and dated a string of what I told Win were men of no possibility but I listened with feigned interest when Ellen told me about a new romance. Apparently, Dave reminded Ellen of Bruce Willis.

"How long have you been seeing him now?"

Ellen shrugs, "I don't know…a while."

After lunch, I walk home and stand facing the four-family flat where I live with Win. Our flat is on the first floor. The other three flats are occupied by elderly couples who'd lived in the building for years, decades really. Win tends the small back yard. When the Barkowskys, the Smiths, and the Carrolls barbeque in the backyard, they invite us to join them as a reward for keeping the yard so nice. Sometimes we do, eating the pork ribs, potato salad, slaw and lime Jello until we excuse ourselves saying we want to catch a movie or that we need to run errands. It's like living in a house full of grandparents, I tell him; more like an old folks home, Win says.

Mrs. Barkowsky is scrubbing the front porch steps as I walk across the street and up the stairs to our flat. "I'm so sorry, Mrs. Barkowsky! I don't mean to spoil your hard work!"

Mrs. Barkowsky gently mutters and wipes where I have just stepped.

Inside, I look for signs that Win has been home. I check the shower, touch the television and the computer to see if they are warm, and look in the closet for his running shoes. I check the refrigerator for a note but only mine is there.

It is almost five when Mrs. Smith rings the doorbell. I have been watching the ballgame on television, eating Doritos from the bag. It is the bottom of the seventh. Mrs. Smith has come to ask me if I would mind walking Louie, her non-descript dog. Win has been gone nine hours now and I agree to walk the dog so that I can trace Win's usual route. I drop my cell phone into my pocket, attach Louie's leash, and head down Mill Street toward Tower Grove Park.

The day is already beginning to cool and the sun is in a good place to make the old, run-down neighborhood have an air of golden beauty. I can hear kids playing in their backyards. An occasional person passes on the sidewalk carrying a newspaper or a small bag of groceries.

I won't find anything, I say, not realizing, at first, that I've spoken out loud. Then, to myself, he won't be laying next to some crime scene tape, no paramedic working feverishly over him, no hit and run victim. He's been gone nine hours. I tried to call him three times during the day. After the third message, I didn't try anymore.

I walk the paved paths of Tower Grove Park. There are some runners but mostly strollers like me, some with a dog, some without. It's a nice evening to walk in the park. The honeysuckle is deeply comforting. I can hear the sound of a basketball thumping on the court behind the stand of trees. A young man and woman share a picnic near the pond. They've brought wine glasses.

I return Louie to Mrs. Smith who wants to chat a bit, but I tell her I must put dinner on. I don't put dinner on, of course. I have no appetite. I don't really know whether to feel angry or fearful—angry that Win has let the day pass without letting me know where he is or fearful that something really has happened to him, something mysterious like alien abduction. I feel almost certain that I haven't married someone as cowardly as my own father, someone who would leave with only the clothes on his back as though he'd be home again in an hour, ready to spend that day and the next day, and the next with his wife. It's now eight o'clock: twelve hours. There is a dream waiting for me to dream it, but it's too early to go to bed. Instead, I take a bath.

Even in summer, I like the bathwater hot enough to turn my skin red and I like to see the steam coming up from the water when I sink into it. I add a touch of salts that smell like eucalyptus and mint. I sink into the water until it covers my shoulders, then my neck, and then my entire head. I lift my face from the water to stare at the ceiling. My hair floats and fans out around my head like seaweed. I stay there until the water grows cold.

What am I to do? Is it crazy at this point to call his parents? Would they be frantic and think I'm foolish for not having called sooner or would they be confused that I had called when there is nothing to tell? It would, after all, look odd that I have let so many hours go by without calling hospitals or the police. My mother did that. Called my father's friends, called hospitals, called the police. How pathetic she looked, dialing number after number, each time growing more frantic until she could hardly speak, until tears streamed down her face, until she had no one left to call. I was only twelve but I'd figured it out. He's not coming back, I'd told her. But she just looked at me and looked through the address book for a number she hadn't yet tried. No, if I called Win's parents, they would surely think that something is terribly wrong between us. I don't call Win's parents; I don't call the hospitals or the police.

I put on my light summer sleeping gown. I pull the blanket to the foot of the bed and slip in under the sheet. Anyone would think it would be impossible to sleep but I am a lover of sleep.

There is an independence to sleeping that makes me adore it. It's as if I'm a craftsman making the best sleep, the best dream I can. I feel famous for it, known far and wide, envied for having mastered the art of the dream.

I like the solitude of sleep, too. There I am, in my own bed, sound asleep, my busy brain telling me a story of me. Even with Win next to me, I am alone in sleep. I am never alone when I am awake even if there is no one with me. It's as though "the other" never ceases to watch, as though I am perpetually observed. But, in sleep, there is no "other." I look at myself; I speak to myself. A dream is like silently reading a good book, but a book penned by the dreamer that gets written and read in the same moment.

Against the odds, sleep is sudden.

I'm on a balcony looking out at the starry, moonlit sky. There is a warm breeze that gently blows my gown around me. And then I feel it. I feel myself rising, lifting up and I am at once terrified and thrilled. I am drawn up even though I want to resist. I am lifted on invisible hands above the houses and trees and I can see the lights outlining the street below. I'm borne away. Borne away from Earth and its woes, borne away from my life and its mysteries, born away from Win and Ellen and the neighbors. The lights on the earth grow dimmer and dimmer. I am carried away.

Siberia

Martin looks back to smile at me; walking two steps ahead, he takes my hand and leads me as we follow our taxi driver along the railroad tracks to the train station entrance marked *Intourist*. The morning is gray and everything in sight is a variation on that color save for the dirty, dark green of the trains. It's almost what I'd imagined...this railway station in a small Siberian town...Khabarovsk. It's more cheerless, though; stacks of taped and tied bales are mounded beside the station door. A little girl, alone, a white organza bow the size of a hambone adorning her head, sits astride one of the bales. The building is more dilapidated than I'd imagined with no hint of a proud past, no emblems or statues, no fading frescos, no flags flying. No commerce is taking place. The boarding areas look all but abandoned.

Martin is as relieved as I am that we have come to a place that distracts us from each other. We let the driver take our bags and he leads us through a corridor that looks like the hallway of an old tenement. There's construction rubble half-swept against the wall, an apple core, shredded waxed paper, a wooden plank set like a bench that we pick our way around until we reach a room in the midst of renovation. In this room, high, broad windows freshly washed let in light that shines on a clutter of furniture suspiciously like the cheap wood veneer vanity tables and boudoir chairs that languish in storage rooms of second hand shops in America. Building materials lay in long rows. Ornamental plaster is in piles; the wedding cake ceiling has been taken down in favor of acoustical tile. Our driver leads us past all this to a counter where our tickets will be manually processed, no computers in sight. The only other passenger in the room is a young Japanese man who sits beneath a bright, new Mitsui sign.

Martin and I will be married four years in December. This is the second marriage for both of us and neither of us have particularly high hopes for this one even though we both ultimately want the same things…some clichéd version of the American Dream. We take off from harrowing separate work lives to spend time together in a more or less remote spot with some dim hope of understanding something about our chances for making that happen. The first year, it was Bali. The second, Viet Nam. The third year, we went to Tasmania. This year, our fourth, we're taking the Trans-Siberian Railway from Khabarovsk to the town of Irkutsk on Lake Baikal.

Through an open door, we can see into the main hall of the station where crowds of people stand in line, baggage in hand. They have the look of refugees but are only average Russian rail passengers with ancient suitcases and hobo-like bundles. Whatever reasons there once were for separating foreign passengers from the citizens of Russia died with the Soviet Union. Nonetheless, we peer at each other from adjacent rooms.

Martin says, "They're curious about us." He looks at me grinning. Martin boyishly speaks in flat statements that make his opinions sound like fact. It suggests a kind of intellectual superiority, as though he is an astute observer who somehow sizes up a situation with uncanny accuracy.

"I wonder why they keep us separate," I say. It annoys me that I make everything sound like a question.

Martin gives our driver a pack of Marlboros as a tip. I sit down with the luggage while Martin goes to buy two bottles of water and to take a few photographs. Fifteen minutes later, he returns at the end of a group of American tourists who, Vittel tucked tightly under their arms, are being shuttled off to their soft class compartments. They eye us and smile; some wave or speak. Martin and I hang back. Remote is getting harder to find. This small, elite herd of American tourists, no doubt, took the package tour from Alaska. We'd hoped to avoid groups like these. Some of the men and women wear polo shirts with Bank of America in white letters over the left breast pocket. The men are strikingly like Martin and like my first husband, Marshall. When Marshall, a banker, divorced me, I married Martin, a corporate tax attorney. That fact still gives me pause. There's a sense of doom about it, like trading a Dalmatian with a thousand spots for one with a thousand and one.

"Let's go," Martin says, picking up his bags. His voice reeks with anticipation and dread, confidence and apprehension. There is courage and enthusiasm in it that both offends and thrills me.

"Yes, shall we go?" I say picking up my bag.

We walk outside along the train platform to hard class car #4, enter the train and find compartment #2. Our cabin floor and fold-down table are littered with eggshells and spots of goo that look like jam. A thin, grimy mattress and pillow are rolled up at the end of the padded leather benches on either side of the cabin. Two more bunks fold down from the wall over the benches. Martin straps the top bunk up against the wall. Faded cotton print curtains hang on a string across the grimy window.

Martin is turning in circles in the small cabin. I stand behind him, then in front of him as he turns, waiting for him to settle. As Martin faces me for the third time, his face brightens. "Sorry," he says over my head, "just give us a minute."

It's the Japanese man from the waiting room. He's left standing in the train corridor, his backpack and gym bag blocking the way to other passengers.

"Under," he says gesturing with his chin. "Space is under." His accent is heavy but we understand him.

Frowning, Martin lifts the bench and stows our bags, drops the seat and we sit cross-legged to give our roommate access. Martin wets his handkerchief with spit and begins to rub at the goo on our table. The Japanese man first checks his ticket against the cabin number and then the berth number, unpacks a few things, stows the rest and then turns to present Martin with his business card, an unreadable squiggle of Japanese characters.

Martin looks at the card, turns it over, and hands it to me.

"I'm Martin," he says, extending his hand, "and this is my wife Nealy."

I look up and smile. Although the man is tall for an Asian, Martin is a head taller and just as lean as the Japanese.

"Akio," the Japanese man says shaking Martin's extended hand.

Akio is definitely younger than we are, probably no more than twenty-five. Martin and I have the wear of failed marriages and stressful jobs, of indecision and pessimism, while Akio seems fresh, his spirit in full bloom.

When the train starts to move, the three of us leave our cabin and stand, forearms resting against the sill of the sooty window, watching the train station and Khabarovsk fade from view. It takes only a few minutes to move from town to the countryside. We are going west toward Eastern Europe on a train that will eventually reach Moscow. We pull down the window and let the air rush into our faces. Suddenly, the somber dinginess of the town falls away. Outside the window, trees edge a flat and winding stream. The air is vibrant, the sky tinged with blue; the green expanse of the dense forest is broken only by the vertical white lines of birch trees.

No more than a minute later, down the train corridor, comes a woman practically as wide as the corridor itself. She is dressed in a worn and stained blue uniform, the blouse of which is too small so gaps between buttons expose both yellowed bra and doughy-white flesh. Her unkempt hair is dyed a brassy reddish-brown and when she smiles she shows us four gold teeth. She is the car matron, the absolute authority over her tiny mobile kingdom. She motions for Martin and me to step inside our cabin; we follow her command and sit across from her. Her Russian is peppered with German and a little English. She calls me Fraulein. We understand from her that clean sheets and towels can be gotten for twenty-five rubles each--about fifteen cents. She takes our ticket, placing it in her book destination-side up, takes the fifty rubles Martin hands her, and returns in a few minutes with our linens.

We are traveling through the southern edge of Far East Siberia. The river that runs through Khabarovsk serves as a border with China somewhere far out of town. We will come to a place on our trip where we are only miles from Mongolia. At the moment, there is little outside our window but the crystalline lakes of melted snow.

I don't know how readily people take on the characteristics of a landscape, but it's true that Martin and I were wildly sexual in Bali that first year, syncing with the incredibly sensuous environment, the heat, and the passionflowers that dripped from our balcony. We lay on the beach almost naked in each other's arms, everything around us smelling of honey and shining with gold light. Everybody is happy in Bali. But this landscape, powerful, vast, unyielding, lays a panorama before us that distances me from Martin in an unexpected way.

The few towns we pass are clusters of no more than a hundred dwellings, spacious whole log homes built by the grandfather or great-grandfather of the current resident. Often the bright paint of the patterned shutters has weathered to mellow oranges, blues, and greens against the aged brown wood. Vegetable gardens, sprinkled with summer flowers, cover the acre or more on which the house sits. There are no paved roads in the towns and we see no cars parked on lawns or traversing the dirt roads. We see no farm equipment, no tractors next to the barns, no trucks. In places, there are wooden sidewalks like the towns of the old West. Except for television antennae and electrical lines, the villages look unchanged for centuries. The houses are primitive but fierce, formidable. They're like handsome and terrible old men...men of character and enduring strength. The towns are few and far between and the train doesn't stop at any of them.

But after several hours, we do stop at a station. Ivan the Terrible, the name we've given to the car matron, stands at the end of the car. Other passengers begin to get off and we follow. When we reach Ivan, she pins us down with her stare and warns us, "sein minuten." Martin and I walk toward a wooden pergola about fifteen feet from the train. There is no station in sight—only the pergola under which women who have brought their goods in baby carriages sell bread, berries, boiled eggs, unsealed bottles of cow-fresh milk and perogies.

"There were so many gardens, Martin...where're all the fresh vegetables?"

"Ummm," grunts Martin. "No doubt the fresh stuff is pickled for winter." He points to perogies stacked in a baby carriage. "These will do," he tells the stout woman showing her four fingers. She picks up a sheet of newspaper, whirls it into a cone, and plops the perogies inside. The sign on her bucket indicates five rubles each.

I would ask Martin what he thinks about the landscape impacting personal relationships but that kind of conversation is too hypothetical for him. When conversations are too hypothetical, he's unable to speak in declarative sentences. It would only frustrate him and he would sigh a lot and concern himself that I am too abstract. Conversations in which he doesn't make statements and I don't ask questions, the kind in which we both make statements, are, in general, arguments.

"Those women looked like lumberjacks, didn't they, Martin?" I say heading back toward the train.

"Yeah, very tough. Survival depends on it. Remember that this is summer when there're fresh vegetables and mild temperatures. Just imagine the winter!"

"So, we're about ten-train-days away from Moscow here? Doesn't it strike you that communism really has no meaning here? Or democracy either for that matter?"

"Just to live...whatever it takes to live...that's the politics."

I wonder if communist couples have communist marriages, the political philosophy transferring its values to personal life: from each spouse according to ability, to each spouse according to need. For Martin and me, a capitalist couple, it's more like, what's good for General Motors is good for America. Martin is General Motors; I am America. Martin is too big to fail.

The train stops again about nine p.m. Now, we've been glued to the window for about seven hours. We have eaten our perogies, which turned out to be fried bread dough stuffed with mashed potato. We washed it down with bottled water. At this stop, a fourth passenger is added to our compartment, a young Russian girl who is apologetically forewarned by Ivan that she'll be sharing sleeping quarters with two Americans and a Japanese. The girl comes in eating seeds from the center of a freshly picked sunflower. She appears to be about seventeen years old, blonde, shy, and smiling reluctantly. Pretty in a Russian peasant sort of way. She's thin and wears black jeans and a white blouse.

We introduce ourselves and she nods, not attempting to repeat our names. When she tells us her name, it is a tangle of unpronounceable Ts and Ws but we each give it a try. She motions for Akio to stand so that she can lift the seat to stow her bag. Then, using the bench for a step, she reaches for a knob over the window and turns on the radio. She reseats herself and picks at the center of the sunflower; it looks as though she is eating the stuffing of a pincushion.

Siberian summer days do not end until at least ten p.m. Then, the absence of industrial smoke, airplane emissions, and car exhaust allows the night sky to exhibit the glories of a magnificent white moon and millions of stars. It's like a time before the industrial revolution. These scattered villages are populated with fishermen and hunters; they cook and warm themselves with wood burning stoves. They trade fur pelts or wild meat and fish to the woman who bakes bread or makes jam. This is the way life is lived in Siberia.

The radio and lights go off automatically at eleven and all four of us go to bed in our clothes. The two men take the bottom bunks and the women take the top. Under the cover, I pull off my bra through the sleeve of my T-shirt and slip off my jeans. I suspect we all sleep badly, with the train jerking and stopping and the bright moon shining through the half-covered window. Still, the clicking of the wheels down the track lulls us to sleep eventually. We have been on the train about twelve hours now and have seen little beyond the exquisite landscape and a few small villages. I know that the train will continue to travel all night through the lush forests that look so rich and past the towns that look so poor.

In the bottom bunk, I hear Martin begin to breathe deeply and evenly. He is basically a good man and tries in his own way to please me but is burdened by the constraint of unfailingly putting himself first. It's something he thinks I should understand. We have a kind of trickle-down marriage.

I am first up in the morning. I tug on my jeans, grab my toilet kit and slip out the door. I'm hoping to get to the bathroom while it is reasonably odor-free from the night's disuse. The stainless steel toilet flushes onto the track and the stainless sink is fed water from an overhead tank. A hole in the middle of the floor allows the car matron to throw a bucket of water across the floor to clean it. It puzzles me that it should smell so bad.

As soon as I leave the toilet compartment, though, I am again mesmerized by the Russian landscape. We have come into some mountains that have a stream winding along their base. The morning mist rises from the land and settles into the mountain gaps. It's hard to remember when I've seen anything quite as beautiful. The pristine stream, the quality of the water looking clear enough to drink, and the evergreen covered mountains lift me up. It would be nice to stay by the stream for a while but the train moves on.

Martin staggers out of the cabin and makes his way to the toilet, which is now occupied. He waits, kit in hand, looking mournful like he always does when he has to wait.

He loves tedium but only certain kinds. This kind requires patience. He likes the kind that requires diligence. On his way back, he kisses the back of my neck. "Let's go to the dining car," he says.

"Are you hungry?" I ask.

Second marriages are always more hesitant than first ones. There's the whole question of love and its betrayals when a first marriage ends. Somewhere in the last four years, Martin and I had settled for commitment, for even insincere loving behavior as a reasonable stand-in for love in capital letters. No one ever quite trusts the second time.

Martin takes my hand and I follow him along the treacherous trail to the dining car several cars in front of ours. In the connections between the cars, we see the tracks whizzing by beneath us. We cross from one car to the next on a metal strip less than a foot wide. Martin releases one door only when, tightening his grasp on my hand, he steps outside the car and is securely attached to the handle of the next. Each car varies slightly in its atmosphere. Each car matron's standards leave her mark. The soft class cars smell of air freshener. Their windows are cleaner. Inside the cabins, I see crocheted doilies on the backs of the seats.

When we open the dining car door, every seat is taken. The Americans welcome us thinking we are part of their group. The tables are loaded down with brown bread, jam and butter, boiled eggs, porridge, and coffee. A waitress shoos us out with a wave of her hand. "One hour!" she yells. "Come back one hour!" But after a bad night's sleep, just the thought of returning from the dining car to our own compartment without having procured breakfast makes me feel defeated, makes me feel naive, brings home the class difference. No, two arduous trips to the dining car in an hour would be too much. Martin gives the waitress a wave of his hand and smiles. He is furious.

Outside Ivan's closet-sized room at the end of the car is a hot water tank with a spigot. I'm just about to get some hot water, congratulating myself that I had thought to bring packets of instant coffee, when the matron comes down the corridor toting two glasses of tea that she gives to me and Martin along with sugar cubes wrapped in paper bearing the picture of a train. We are grateful and trot into our cabin to ravage our supply of peanut butter crackers, a parting gift from my sister who dropped us at the airport. I return the cups with a gift of a large chocolate bar and although she seems pleased, I get the impression this is not the reward she is after.

The relentless beauty of the landscape passes our window like a constant travelogue. We eat, doze, and look out the window to watch the infinite blue sky and endless green landscape. By noon, Akio and Martin are playing chess on a small magnetic board Akio brought. I read an article about Marilyn Monroe in *Vanity Fair*. The Russian girl sign languages Martin out of his iPod and taps her foot to the music. Then the train stops. Stops in the middle of nowhere. Stops dead center in the middle of nowhere. The Russian girl doesn't notice but just bobs her toe to the music.

Then, we hear Ivan booming in and out of each compartment, shaking passengers out of their bunks and off the train. When she storms into ours, Akio picks up his bag but Ivan grabs it and throws it back down onto the seat. "Nyet!" she warns him. We are allowed to take nothing. She gives Akio a little nudge on the shoulder and tugs at the foot of the Russian girl to get her moving; then off she rampages to the next cabin.

We are herded off, rushing toward the narrow exit as though the train were on fire. Outside, passengers stand in little clusters not straying far from the tracks. Through the window, I see two uniformed men in the first cabin going through luggage, stripping away bedding, looking in, under, and around. One uniform closes the curtains all along the side of the train. Our Russian roommate saunters off toward the end of the train still connected to Martin's iPod. The family from the next compartment sighs and sits down in the grass. The man pulls out a pocketknife and begins to pare his fingernails. From the front of the train, a man in a Bank of America shirt strolls toward us, looking at Martin. When he reaches Martin, he stops. He's rolling a toothpick around in his mouth and jingling change in his pockets.

"Any idea what's happening?" he asks Martin. The man has a vise-grip on his calm demeanor. He reeks of the golf course at Hilton Head.

"Looks like they're searching for something." Martin too is determined to be nonchalant. He shoves his hands into his pockets in the same way as the man he faces.

The man spits his toothpick to the ground, sucks his teeth, and runs change through his fingers.

"Any idea what?"

Martin shakes his head. "Not even an educated guess."

"Ya'all traveling alone?" He glances briefly my way. Martin nods.

"Going all the way to Moscow?"

"Only as far as Lake Baikal."

"Well..." he says, sucking his teeth and nodding. He shrugs, turns, and heads back toward a woman standing in the distance looking anxiously in his direction.

Martin and I have begun to share experience in very separate ways. I see Martin standing there next to the train door, looking at his watch, already out of patience. He begins ducking and bobbing his head to try to see into the train windows, shifting his weight from one foot to the other and I can almost feel his mind buzzing with the frustration of unanswered questions, with the offense of invaded privacy, with the nauseating effect of having no power. When I think of spending my life with this man, getting old with him, I feel deeply bereft.

The second year we were married, we were crossing an ochre river in Viet Nam. The flat raft of a ferry was crowded with the kind of men we'd seen everywhere in that country. Cavernous lines gave character to their faces. Rough, callused feet were exposed in plastic sandals. A lean and browned man squatting next to me reached slowly toward my hand and drew it near him to examine. My hand was deadly white in his dark, rough ones. I wore a thin gold ring and bracelet.

In Viet Nam, our lack of calluses qualified us as nobility. We had stopped being the enemy long ago. Martin and I walked the streets like victors, proudly, hand in hand, eating our meals at the Metropole, buying without negotiating. We made love as though we were good at it, better at it than the cyclo-driver who peddled us all the way across Hanoi for a dollar. Still, after two years, Martin and I knew no more about our prospects for happiness and stability than the day we'd married.

Down toward the front of the train where the soft class cars are, tablecloths are spread on the grass for the American tour group. Bottles of water, bowls of fruit and plates of brown bread and meat are being set out. We've been waiting an hour. It's past lunch. I sit in the grass and pretend to look for four leaf clovers. Martin strides over and tries to re-board the train, the entry of which is guarded by Ivan. I hear him yelling, But our food is in there! Can't I even get something to eat? Ivan stretches her thick arms, barring Martin's way. Oh, for Christ's sake, I hear him mutter as he turns away.

"Want to go down to where the other Americans are?" I ask when he returns. He sits down heavily in the grass beside me. "I'm sure they'd share if you're hungry."

Martin doesn't answer. It's not so much that he wants food as that he wants *his* food. He plants his elbows on his knees and glares into the scrub preceding the dense forest just beyond the space cleared beside the tracks. It isn't possible to talk now. I'm not in the mood to cajole him. I look around to see Akio stretching his legs, trying to speak to other passengers; he has brought a giant bag of candy to hand out to the children. The Russian girl is nowhere in sight. The sun is warm and I stretch out, lying back in the stiff grass.

After two hours of waiting, we are allowed to re-board. The seats have been lifted and our luggage searched, our bags left open. Our linens, mattresses and pillows have been tossed onto the floor. Akio returns with us and emits a sigh of relief to learn that he isn't missing anything. None of us are. Even our stashes of cash are intact. At the far end of our car, Ivan finishes replacing metal panels in the corridor wall.

Martin and I once again stand at the window next to Akio.

"It is common...common?" he considers the word, "usual...ah...usual that European and American couples travel husband and wife, desu ne?"

"Yes," Martin answers.

"Not so usual for Japanese. Husbands travel with...uh...what you call fellow company men. Wives travel with other ladies." He looks at us questioningly. "Why American man travel with his wife?"

Martin laughs. "I wouldn't want to go on vacation with the guys I work with! I get enough of them at the office."

"I think, Akio," I say leaning past Martin and looking at Akio, "that it's important for a husband and wife to share experience so that later in life they can reminisce." It embarrasses me to say this in front of Martin. It feels like a lie.

"Reminisce?" The word puzzles Akio.

"Recall pleasant times," I explain

"Ahhh! Americans have Christian marriage?"

Martin laughs again, throwing back his head this time. "Hardly, Akio. I was raised a Jew but I'm what you might call a lapsed Jew, if there is such a thing. Non-practicing anyway. Nealy, well, she's a lapsed Protestant is it? Or Catholic?" Martin gives me a questioning look. "Anyway, some lapsed thing or another. Christian marriage? I don't think so!"

"It's more a capitalist marriage than a Christian one, Akio." I say not really being prepared to explain that.

"Well, anyway," Akio says, "I would like someday to be a couple like you!"

Akio stands two windows down seemingly absolutely aching at the beauty of the landscape and I wonder if there is such a thing as too beautiful, too peaceful. In an odd way, we have been humbled and cleansed by the acts of the uniformed invaders. Some tension that we didn't even know was there is relieved or perhaps redirected. We were violated, cleared of suspicion, and found to be innocent of some treachery we couldn't even conceive.

Even though it's fairly late afternoon, we decide to journey to the dining car once more. With the American tour group having been fed, Martin and I may have a chance at getting served. The trip from our car to the dining car is no less daunting than the first time we made it. When we arrive, we sit down at a booth and wait. A woman standing at the front of the car is filling the napkin holders, first cutting the napkins in half. We eat a salad of diced cucumbers and boiled potatoes with an oil dressing and fried bread and jam, a lunch that reminds me of *The Grapes of Wrath*. I'm thinking of Rose'a'shar'n mixing flour and water and frying it in bacon fat. Martin orders tea and I decide to risk coffee. I am brought a demitasse of murky liquid not quite coffee-color. The taste is not bad, though, once I strain the grounds through my teeth. As we sit there, the train once again comes to a station and stops. There is the same gathering as at other stations, the women under a wooden shelter with their goods, women with buckets of perogie or boiled potatoes sold in newspaper cones. The train's cook signals a farmer who carries a bucket of berries. The cook dumps them into a cardboard box and returns the bucket to the farmer. I imagine berry pies, pancakes, and muffins and wonder what the tatted and T-shirted cook plans to do to delight the soft class passengers.

No bill is offered to us and when Martin asks how much we owe, the waiter hesitates a moment and then asks for three American dollars. It is more than we've paid for larger meals in Khabarovsk but less than we'd paid for a single cup of espresso in New York. There is no doubt that the American dollars go into the Russian waiter's pocket without a moment's thought to his employers.

The night passes not unlike the previous one. Martin and Akio play chess. The train stops, passengers get off to buy dinner, then re-board. The Russian girl, sulky and uncommunicative, usurps Martin's iPod. The train is beginning to feel confining. We all seem desperate to stretch our limbs, to breathe air not tainted with engine fumes. We long for the train to stop long enough for us to get off, walk up and down the train tracks, feel the grass, feel the sun on our face.

Martin and I will leave the train tomorrow morning when we reach Lake Baikal so our car matron's marketing efforts increase. After lunch, as we come through the door at the end of the car, Ivan sees us and approaches us excitedly. Chattering away, she takes Martin's arm and turns him toward the train window inside our compartment. What had been a milky profusion of dirty clouds now sparkles with bright clarity.

"Reward!" she beams. In half English-German-Russian, half charades, we understand that she is given "extra points" by the uniforms for the presence of American tourists but that the presence of the Japanese had earned her nothing. The clean window is her treat for us. Martin mutters that it is too little too late. Ivan cocks her head to one side and motions for us to follow her into her small office. The room is no more than a closet with dials and controls covering one wall. The three of us in the room almost touch noses. She has an array of silver glass holders, the kind we'd used our first morning on the train. She wants five American dollars for each for them. They have Sputnik embossed on all but one and that one has a Napoleon-esque male figure on it. I decide on two of them and Martin hands her ten dollars. Enthused by our response, she next shows us a bottle of vodka. "Putin" she says pretending to down a shot, "Medvedev" she says making the motion again. She writes seventeen American dollars on a scrap of paper. She explains, motioning with her hands and scribbling down $300, that she wants to go to America and she needs only three hundred more American dollars. We pretend to be pleased that she is interested in coming to America but decline her offer to sell us vodka. She knows her opportunity for capitalist interaction with us is coming to a close.

After a little more than fifty hours on the train, our cabin is littered with berries, cracker crumbs, and a half bottle of water. In the bottom of the clear green glass of the bottle, which sits in the sun of the window, brown fuzz floats. Martin's iPod has disappeared from the ears of our Russian roommate. When he tries to question her, she pretends to understand nothing. Martin shrugs and tells me he figures she'll return it when it runs out of juice. He brought a charger and adapter but there is no way to use it on the train.

At a long stop at a station, we opt to buy nothing, feeling that our time aboard the train is now limited and it is safe to deplete our supply of coffee, peanut butter crackers, California raisins, and almonds. Surely the Intourist food at Lake Baikal will be better than the food on the train—at least the food served to the hard class passengers.

Sometimes the Russian girl locks us all out of our cabin. We think only that she is changing clothes or craving a moment alone. Once though, as we are all lolling about reading, she stealthily removes our binoculars from her bag and places them on the floor then scoots them with her foot a few inches in our direction. It is unlikely that Martin will see his iPod again without a fight. We sit amid our bag of food, binoculars, cameras, books, magazines and clothes that spill obscenely across our side of the car while the Russian girl sits eating her boiled egg and sunflower seeds. Later, she walks down the corridor and strikes up a conversation with an Asian-looking girl with bleached hair and a definite black eye.

There are children in the car who shyly steal glances at us and one little boy who flirts outrageously and talks to us not in the least puzzled that we respond with words he can't understand. He smiles and we give him a small chocolate bar. Shortly, he returns with a peach for us.

The day passes, then the night. By morning, I awake to find myself alone in the compartment. In a few hours, Martin and I will be on solid ground again. I'm not sorry to move on from the train to the open space of Lake Baikal. My guess is that Martin has gone to the bathroom but then I see his kit on his bunk. I pull on my clothes and gather my own kit to head for the bathroom myself. The corridor is empty but, when I try the bathroom door, it's locked, so I move down the corridor a bit to stand and wait. I open the window and am immediately refreshed by the breeze.

I hear the lock of the toilet compartment click and see Martin suddenly standing in the corridor, his hand still resting on the compartment door handle.

"Nealy," He starts as if he's about to tell me something, but then he jerks his head as a signal for me to follow him. He takes my arm and turns me toward our compartment door.

"Martin, I really have to pee. It'll only take a second." But Martin has hold of my arm and is not letting go. "Martin? What's going on?"

As Martin pushes me toward our cabin, the bathroom door opens again and the Russian girl steps out. She is looking down, checking and smoothing her clothes, touching the edges of her mouth; then she looks up. Seeing me, she steps back in and closes the door again.

"What's going on?" I demand but he doesn't answer. He and I go into our cabin, close the door, and wait silently for the Russian girl to pass by on her way to anywhere besides our compartment. After she is out of sight, I rush to the bathroom myself. I stand in the middle of the toilet compartment listening to the train clack down the track.

In the third year of our marriage, we took a trip to Tasmania, stopping first in Australia and then taking a short flight from Sidney to Hobart. What I remember most about Tasmania was the horrifying number of kangaroos and wallabies that had been hit by cars and left to rot on the roads. We'd visited a zoo to see the Tasmanian Devils and watched the zookeeper throw the leg of road-killed kangaroo into a den of Devils.

Martin and I silently drove the dusty roads of Tasmania dodging carcasses of dead animals. The lovemaking that had been part of Bali and Viet Nam had disappeared in Tasmania, maybe because we had now been married three years or maybe because of the bloody landscape that surrounded us. On the fourth day into our vacation, I came down with something and spent the day in bed while Martin spent the day sightseeing by himself. He seemed somehow cheered by his time alone.

Standing in the john of a moving train in the middle of Siberia, I realize I had let too many things slide. I am forty-four years old, this is my second marriage, and I am entrenched in a pattern of powerlessness, at least regarding Martin. Going back into the corridor of the train, I see Martin looking out the window. The Russian girl now occupies the cabin. She is winding the cord of Martin's charger and tucking it and the adapter into her bag.

Martin wants to get coffee and I follow behind him, across the death-defying metal bridges between railroad cars. We sit in a booth across from each other.

"Are you going to tell me what you were doing in the bathroom with our little Russian room mate?" I purse my lips and raise my eyebrows wondering why am I even asking what I already know.

"I wasn't in the bathroom with her," he says flatly. "I don't know what you think you saw, but I wasn't in the bathroom with that girl."

The Bill Clinton Maneuver. Then we don't speak. I don't know what I've come to expect from a man, from a husband, or what I've come to accept. What politics and economics apply in a marriage when love is no longer part of the equation? What can be done when the power is not meted out in equal portions? When there is legal union but not equal partnership within the union? What would happen if I spoke in declarative sentences? Would Martin default to asking questions?

Later, back in our cabin, Akio and Martin are asleep, books open on their chests. The Russian girl is plugged into what used to be Martin's iPod. Across the back of it, in red nail polish, she has written something I guess is her name. The train car seems smaller than before...more confining...more stifling.

I gaze out the window in our cabin continually awed by the scale of this somber country. Summer in Siberia lacks the frivolity of summer in California. In Siberia, summer is hustle, a fevered rush to harvest, a respite from the bitterness of winter. It is not the idleness of a lazy afternoon spent by the pool. Surviving the winter means capitalizing on summer.

Through the window, I see farmers cutting hay, using scythes and piling the hay on long poles to be dragged away. They work in groups; some look like families, and when the hay is in ricks, they sit under a tree together and rest. Sometimes a cloth is spread and covered with bottles of wine and loaves of bread. We see a truck hauling the hay less often than we see a horse and wagon. Only once in a thousand miles have we seen a tractor. The image of three Russian men rhythmically swinging their scythes remains with me when I close my eyes.

From the direction of our door, Ivan is hissing and motioning me to step outside. She takes my arm and practically presses me against the train window.

"Baikal," she says smiling. I gasp...literally, gasp. Before me is an expanse of water surprising even in this country of overwhelming vistas. It is the largest fresh water lake in the world, some four hundred miles long, forty miles across and a mile deep. It looks like a sea. Martin and Akio rouse themselves and step out into the corridor. The lake comes in and out of view, the railroad tracks at times almost on the shore of the lake and then falling back behind trees. We stand speechless, waiting for the next glimpse. I look at Akio whose eyes are glossy, near tears. Since he was ten years old, it had been his dream to ride this train, he tells us. "When I see the lake," he says, "I am so impressed, I can not express my feeling."

We pass a group of people swimming who wave to the passing train. Some boys, maybe eleven or twelve years old, playing on a rock on the shore make us laugh when they pull down their pants and show us their bare behinds. We are still perhaps an hour from the end of our journey. The car matron makes one last capitalist advance, offering us a white shawl for twenty dollars. When we decline, she brings us tea and pins wings on our T-shirts. The wings are emblems that we've been passengers on the Trans-Siberian Railway, she tells us. When I return the empty cups, I give her five American dollars. She smiles—American cash is the reward she's been waiting for.

The train again stops for no apparent reason and again we wait for it to start up. There are only a few small fishing boats on the lake. No resort hotels dot the shores. The water is so clear that we can see the bottom of the lake near the shore from the train window.

Then I say, not expecting to, "The Siberian landscape makes me sad."

Martin frowns. He tears his gaze away from the view to look at me. "I thought you said it was beautiful!"

I nod. I keep my eyes on him even after he turns away.

He is agitated, of course. He has his own fears.

There is a tremendous loneliness about the silent landscape, and a kind of terror too, as though the winter could suddenly replace the summer, freezing everything to stone and covering everything with snow until even the train disappears.

The tracks have drifted away from the lake and Martin looks hard through the trees to see if he can still catch some glimpse of it. Then, he goes back into our cabin. Most passengers have left their bunks to huddle in the corridor and, like me, look out the window. A few, those not going on to Moscow, already have their luggage ready at their feet. Martin raises the seat and begins to gather our belongings. He takes my bag from storage and sets it on the floor. He stuffs my magazine into the side pocket. Martin glances at the Russian girl who ignores him, her eyes cast down.

The town of Irkutsk is beginning to show signs of its existence. Log houses are giving way to apartment blocks. Paved roads are beginning to appear. Cars and busses become more frequent. The train is moving very slowly now and it is a matter of minutes before we arrive at the train station.

I direct my stare to the Russian girl. "Martin," I say, "your iPod?"

"She doesn't have much," he says pulling our bags into the corridor. "Let her have it. I'll get another one when we get home."

Relationships are impacted by how commerce is carried out, what the goods are, how things are bartered. There is a simultaneous poverty and richness about Siberia that has to do with the richness of the land and it's stubbornness in yielding that richness to the people who live there, in yielding it to the young Russian girl. There is no generosity about Siberia, no gentleness, only a demand that life be lived harshly amidst the gift of the landscape's splendor.

    When we arrive at the station, Martin wrestles our bags off the train and moves them out of the way of the other passengers. He looks small standing there surrounded by our immodest luggage. Still, with the low covering over the platform, the station squarely behind it and Irkutsk laying itself out behind that, we are moving into a landscape of a more civilized dimension.

Misogi Harae

I

Boisterous Germans play cards in the back of a train that speeds along the tracks between Tokyo and Hiroshima. The snap of the cards and the laughter drift up to Karen sitting alone in the front of the car. She doesn't look back at them even though she smiles. Instead, she looks at the empty seat meant for her father. Struggling a little to keep her hands from reaching out to that empty space, she realizes in that moment that "alone" has degrees, has infinite depth, and now she feels the fullness and gravity of it, a deep and utter "alone." A card smacks down, laughter follows. Karen doesn't smile this time, keeps her hands in her lap, and watches the countryside appear then vanish as the train enters then leaves each little village along the route.

Between Karen and the Germans, Japanese business men softly snore and mothers doze while children sleep on their laps. A girl no more than nineteen passes through the car with a lazy-wheeled cart full of soft drinks and rice bowls; the girl's pea green uniform gives her skin a sickly cast. The smell of soy sauce wafts from the girl's cart; a Japanese teenager sitting in back of Karen stirs.

Karen had promised her father. Sure, she had fleeting thoughts of cashing in the tickets to Tokyo and going instead to see the pyramids in Egypt or the elephants in Thailand, but, she promised him. Her father had been part of the reconstruction forces in Japan when she was a child. Of course, she barely remembers. She was two when her family arrived in Tokyo in 1952 and so her memory is not trustworthy. What she recalls is her parents memory inherited. "Karen," her mother would tell her pointing to a photo, "this is you!" The photo is black and white, but Karen remembers the little red coat with a black velvet collar even if she doesn't remember the sweets shop in the background. She vaguely remembers unpaved streets and a house with thin, wooden walls and, she remembers the visit with her father to an ancient teahouse set atop a newly constructed building. Her father was an engineer and Army officer sent to help rebuild the devastated country. In block after block of rubble, astonishingly, sometimes a frail wooden structure would remain untouched. The engineers would respectfully set the structure aside, the miracle of its survival testimony to the gods' favor. Then, when the new building was complete, up the frail structure would be hoisted, up, up, up to the roof. Karen's father took her to see the building he'd been working on. By this time, she was four. There was no elevator, so they walked up five flights of gleaming stairs sliding their hands over brand new handrails. Modern lights seen nowhere else in Tokyo lit their way and the recently painted walls gave a freshness to the building that shut out the smell of smoke that was present everywhere. The stairs led to a door that opened onto the roof where the teahouse sat.

  As she recalls it now, almost fifty years later, she is amazed at the brilliance of that; the traditional architecture not buried or displaced by the new western building, but exalted because the gods had selected this teahouse to survive. She remembers holding her father's hand as they approached the old teahouse and looked through the round, glassless windows to see an interior that looked untouched, looked exactly as it might have before the fire bombs fell.

By the time her family returned to the United States, Japan and the war had her father in its grip. Year after year, he sat behind his desk in a first floor bedroom that had been converted into a home office. As the years passed, he seemed older and smaller behind the growing stacks of paper that covered at first only his desk, then later every inch of floor around it. It grew until the bundles of paper stretched from wall to wall, floor to ceiling. Karen and her brother would crawl through the stacks unseen while their father tallied the dead. Over and over, her father read stories of survival, and every year he looked up statistics of the impact of the atom bomb to see how the numbers had dwindled over time—how many had lived ten years after the bomb, how many fifteen, and on and on. Her father had worked with a team of American and Japanese volunteers to ask survivors to draw pictures of what they had seen. One of the drawings, framed and hanging on the wall behind his desk, showed an inferno from which people, stick figures, were running away screaming.

At age eighty-one and in failing health, her father wanted to see Japan one more time and asked Karen if she would help. He was especially interested in returning to Hiroshima, a place he visited every trip. He exhausted himself easily, now, and needed to sit and catch his breath after only a few yards. Karen had no idea how they would manage. Still, they bought tickets and planned their route—five days in Tokyo and three in Hiroshima plus two travel days. Her father, though, did not live to make the trip.

When the train arrives at the station, Karen glances at the card players. They join a group of German tourists and board a bus while Karen takes a taxi to her hotel to drop off her luggage. Her afternoon is spent wandering around the city, going into shops, sitting in the parks, walking along the river's edge thinking of the picture over her father's desk. On the second day, she goes into the Peace Memorial Museum.

Simply passing through the doors of the museum fills Karen with dread. Her father's life was consumed by the event the museum memorializes and that consuming interest cast its shadow over the entire family. The mushroom cloud always seemed to linger in their house. She remembers, once while she was still in college, meeting her father in a little noodle shop on Queen Anne Hill. He told her, "The victors have the luxury of forgetting…the defeated never do. But we victors must remember too." They ate their noodles; he gave her the un-lacquered chopsticks he'd brought her, "It isn't so much to ask, is it? That the victors observe, bear witness so that they know? It isn't too much."

Karen knows that she will see the exhibits through her father's eyes, hear his voice, and she is terrified that she will fail to feel the full measure of compassion that honest knowing requires. Or, that feeling the full measure, she will buckle under its weight. But, her father is with her, his voice encouraging her, his strength supporting her. The first exhibit contains photos of neighborhoods reduced to ash, some burned, others totally incinerated. The river was on fire with burning people. At first Karen protects herself, puts a distance between seeing and knowing. But when she reaches a small pair of shoes, her defenses collapse. Involuntarily, she gasps, holds her breath, backs away, but the heart-breaking shoes draw her back with their demand to be looked at. She looks closely at every detail. In truth, they look no more than a relic from the era, a curiosity in an expensive antique shop. They are alone in a Plexiglas case. The placard says that the shoes belonged to a schoolboy. Ten years old. He had been on his way to school when the Atom bomb incinerated him. He had evaporated in a flash of light and heat, leaving only his shoes behind. The placard says that the temperature at the point of impact was estimated to be about 540,000 degrees. No, these are not mere artifacts, museum curiosities; these are shoes with provenance.

Shifting her eyes from the shoes to her own image reflected in the Plexiglas, for a split second, she sees her father's reflection beside her own; Karen's face is superimposed over the shoes. Their laces are still woven through the islets and her hollow eyes lay over them like a double-exposed photograph. The shoes are untied as if the child had been blown out of them, but the bomb had not blown him out of his shoes; the intensity of the heat had simply vaporized him.

The crisp air of the museum is suddenly cloying and too thick to breathe. Karen has broken out in a sweat looking at those haunting shoes. She feels seasick on the solid, unwavering hardwood of the museum floor. She finds herself moving lethargically from exhibit to exhibit of twisted eye glasses, of surviving leather school bags, of tin lunch buckets, all possessions of the children on their way to school. Her brain has gone all blurry and she drags her hand along the wooden case to reach the next exhibit. She is pulled into the moment, 8:15 am, August 6, 1946. Enola Gay drops Little Boy and the world changes in a flash of unimaginable heat.

Her father came to see this over and over, standing in front of the absolute horror these cases so neatly and cleanly display. It's as if the chaos of that day is being forced into careful order…as though there is an insistence of control over that which can not be controlled, a mastery over that which can not be mastered--immaculate, tidy cases with artifacts labeled in three languages demanding that the past be managed. She imagines her father among strangers, his face unreadable, appearing to look on only curiously as if the cases contain specimens of butterflies or exotic insects. She tries to focus on the next display case. She's not sure, though, what she is seeing. Her nausea is getting the best of her. She tries to shake the fogginess but that only makes her head swim in dizzy circles so that the captions, in German, English, and Japanese, seem all alike. Her eyes fumble to find the right placard. Then, the words come clear and she reads: "These pictures were taken just days after the bomb was dropped." The passive voice leaves the perpetrator without blame. The pictures show shadows where no person exists to cast them. They are not shadows, of course, but dark stains in human shape. They are the remains of the incinerated, seared into the sidewalk where they fell. Not even charred bones were left.

Her nausea is about to express itself all over the pristine museum floor. The ladies room is just through the open doorway a little down the hall. She tries to be calm, to walk slowly to the door, to breathe deeply. When she gets inside the ladies room, it is empty. Not taking time to close the stall door, she bends over and heaves her lunch into the toilet bowl. Then, she closes the door, flushes the toilet, and drops its seat down. There she sits gasping for air.

This is what Karen knows about death: her only sibling, her brother Kyle, died of leukemia when he was fourteen, her mother, Loretta, died of breast cancer at fifty-seven, her husband, Gary, died at thirty-eight after the car Karen was driving was hit by a speeding police car, and now her father, her last living relative, has passed away at eighty-one. Karen knows something about death and loss: she is reminded with every beat of her heart.

Still, she doesn't regret in the least coming to Japan, burdened as she is by her own grief. She takes comfort in remembering her purpose and begins to breathe. She could have gone to see the giraffes on the Serengeti. She could be riding a tiger in India or canoeing down the rapids in Colorado. But she chose Japan; she knows with certainty, though, that she did not come to this place to sit in a ladies room stall at the Peace Memorial Museum feeling sick, not just to her stomach, but sick, deathly sick at heart.

She splashes cold water on her face. Then she leans on the sink peering into the mirror. Her light blonde hair is disheveled; she combs it with her fingers and tries to pat down poufy spots. Her skin looks doughy white. She pinches her cheeks. Her eyes are red even though she hasn't been crying. She rinses out the foul taste of vomit with a handful of water.

Karen had been too little to understand that she and her family were occupiers when her father had taken her to see that teahouse, but she was not too little to understand that she was privileged in a way that scared her. She knew even then that the children of this country did not have blonde curls like hers, did not have her long legs, did not have dolls, or warm red wool coats with black velvet collars. Her father, a tall man, had towered over the Japanese men and Karen grew to be almost as tall as her father. How did he manage, Karen wondered. How did he do it? How did he come to this place over and over again?

The cold water restores a little color to her face, but fails to revive her. She needs air. She is halfway through the exhibits. If she doesn't see the rest now, she must return the next day. Today, right now, is her last best chance to see what her father saw. Still, it can't be helped. She tries not to rush from the museum, tries not to let her panic show. Still, she lurches past the reception desk not acknowledging the domo arigato and stumbles down the stairs and out onto the sidewalk.

II

Karen takes a deep breath. Down the street a bit from the museum is a coffee shop. She makes her way there and goes in. There are only a few people filling the tables; still trying to catch her breath, she collapses into a chair

When the server comes, Karen squeaks out, "Misu, Kudasai." She rummages through her bag and pulls out her *Lonely Planet* guidebook to hide herself.

"Are you okay?" A man is suddenly standing at her table, apparently speaking to her. He has a heavy accent Karen recognizes as German. She lifts her head and nods.

"I should have known you were American, but at first I thought you might have been on our bus. You're upset," the man says sympathetically. "Is there something I can do?"

He is one of the card-players from the train.

"No, no, I'm perfectly fine." Karen sounds dismissive, even annoyed. She doesn't mean to. She's not fine, but this man is a foreigner and a total stranger. Well, it's Japan; she's a foreigner too. "Why should you have known I'm American?" She does her best to be pleasant, controlling her tone, trying to project friendliness.

"Well, for one thing, your guidebook is in English." He smiles at her. "You don't mind, do you?" he says pulling out the chair across the table but waiting for her permission to sit down. "Tours," he gestures, tilting his head toward the bus. "I hate them."

Karen offers the seat to him with a sweeping hand, glancing behind her at the German tour bus.

"My sister insisted I come. They are 'concerned.'" He kinks his fingers in air-quotes.

He must have been sitting at another table when he saw Karen frazzled and alone because as soon as he is seated the server delivers his coffee and a glass of water for Karen, who then orders coffee too.

"I don't mean to intrude on your solitude." He sips his coffee. "You were visiting the museum?"

Karen nods.

"My sister is something of a disaster junky," the man says, "Pearl Harbor, Auschwitz, Holocaust museums, Lockerbie, Scotland. I didn't used to go with them; my wife didn't like to travel. But now my sister and her husband sort of look after me." He lifts and drops his shoulders in a way that Karen thinks is probably characteristic. There's no mistaking what he means by "but now." "Besides," he continues, "my brother-in-law begged me to come. I think he's a bit weary of disasters himself."

"You went into the museum?" Karen closes her book.

"Barely. Too grim for me." He extends his hand. "I'm Karl," he says.

"Karen." She anticipated a polite, distant handshake but Karl grabs her hand solidly and holds it firmly before he lets go.

"The museum," Karl frowns, "It's important that it exist, I suppose, even if I can't bear it." His face is narrow and what remains of his hair is still blonde. "Death," he continues, "suffering, lives ruined into the next generation—we need to be reminded." He shrugs again then adds, "Well, I *suppose* we need to be reminded. What would happen if we erased our memories of war?" He laughs, stirs his coffee, crosses his legs, and relaxes back in his chair. "Remembering doesn't seem to have done us much good, though, has it?"

Karen looks down into her cup. Then, raising her head to look at him she smiles. "Your English is good. Where did you learn?"

One cup of coffee turns into two. Karl is interesting, easy to be around, so an hour slips by without much notice. Karl is talking about his love for American country and western music and has just begun his version of "Stand by Your Man" in German when he suddenly stands up to greet a trim woman with very short white hair and her companion, a short, round gentleman. The woman seems to be scolding Karl and he, once again, produces a shrug. He introduces the two as his sister, Marilyn, and her husband, Werner. Marilyn smiles, apologizes for her curt remarks to her brother, and takes Karen's hands in both of hers to shake them warmly. She speaks English with less of an accent than Karl but when Werner greets Karen, he does it in German. Werner doesn't know English well; he can understand most of what is said, he tells her haltingly, but can't formulate sentences in English in his head. Their conversation stumbles on, interrupted by Karl or Marilyn's explanations of what Werner is trying to say.

From the minute Marilyn and Werner sit down, Karen likes them. Marilyn is friendly and touches Karen's arm asking where she's from—territory that Karl and Karen have already covered. Werner and Karl, chatting in German, laugh and Karl explains that Werner thinks Japanese coffee is every bit as bad as American coffee.

When Marilyn asks Karen what she thinks of the museum, Karen is already regretful and has to admit that she was so overwhelmed that she hadn't actually seen the entire museum.

"You missed the story of Yamaguchi, then!"

Marilyn draws out a small notebook. Both Werner and Karl throw up their hands protesting loudly so that Marilyn slips the book back into her bag.

When the four of them have finished their coffee, Marilyn invites Karen to walk with them down the wide paths between the Peace Dome and the Peace Memorial and links arms with her as the two men trail behind. It feels new and at the same time familiar. Marilyn talks softly of the places she's been, the horror and the beauty that she's seen.

"Why?" Karen has to ask, "Why do you put yourself through that?"

Marilyn shrugs mimicking the habit of her brother. "It's hard to put into words. Paying a debt? That's not quite it. Something perhaps to do with karma or atonement, or making myself whole?" She sighs, "That doesn't really explain it."

Karen pats Marilyn's arm. "My father used to tell me that we are obligated to know," In her head, she sees herself across from her father in the noodle shop.

"Yes." Marilyn looks back over her shoulder at the two men several yards behind. "You see, our father was in the German army." She looks back again as if she wants to be sure the men are out of earshot. "We don't know what he did during the war. I just remember his terrible nightmares, his rages, his long periods of silence. Post traumatic stress we'd call it today. Then one day," Marilyn clears her throat, "our father shot himself in our own living room."

Karen stops in her tracks but Marilyn pulls her forward.

"I was sitting on the floor right in front of him playing with my dollhouse." Marilyn neither shudders nor stammers. Her eyes watch her feet move forward, one step, another step. "I was maybe six and Karl was just a baby. The neighbor took us away immediately while our mother dealt with the police, with the blood, with my father's body. When the neighbor returned us to our mother a day or two later, my dollhouse was gone. I remember my mother scrubbing the floor and furniture endlessly and then finally dragging the blood-stained chair to the backyard and setting it on fire."

"How awful!" Karen stops again. Marilyn again urges her forward. "How awful for everybody."

When Gary died, Karen didn't see him. He was buried while Karen was still in the hospital. She thought that was hard but now she wonders if it would have been harder to have seen him in his coffin. Karen's arm is still linked with Marilyn's and they begin their slow stroll again.

"We were just small children. I doubt that Karl actually remembers." Marilyn shrugs. "Why do I do it? Karl calls me a disaster junkie! Hah! Maybe I do it to honor the dead. Or maybe to honor life." Marilyn looks again to see how far back her brother and husband are, then Marilyn smiles cheerfully, "It was decades ago and only one death after all. What is that among so many?"

This place where 140,000 were lost in one day, where others suffered for years with their own illnesses, their lost loved ones, their damaged souls, what, indeed, was one death? And yet, Karen knows with total conviction that death, even in masses, is always singular.

The men catch up to them and the conversation gets around to dinner plans and Marilyn invites Karen to join them; they have reservations in a well-known tempura restaurant at the hotel where Karen is staying. They part with a plan to return to their respective hotels to freshen up and rest, then meet again at the restaurant.

At seven, Karen takes the elevator down to the lobby floor. When she steps out of the elevator, Karl smiles, then, placing an arm around her waist, leads Karen to a booth where his sister and brother-in-law are already sipping sake from little blue cups. Karen slides across the maroon leather seat to face Marilyn; Karl slides in beside her. Tall planters of bamboo separate one booth from another giving the place a quiet and private ambiance.

It is inevitable in this city to talk about the events that changed the course of history. Marilyn begins again to enumerate the sites she has visited, everything she has already mentioned, but adds her visit to Gethsemane where Jesus had been crucified. Marilyn ticks off places on her fingers. The Book Depository in Dallas follows Gethsemane.

"A nation's history has a way of becoming personal history," Karen says, partly because the sake is taking affect and partly because she was losing track of the conversation. "My father," Karen says, "was greatly moved by the events here and spent much of his life studying them."

"Studying events or atoning for them?" Marilyn asks.

Karen has to think for a minute. "Well, in my father's mind, I'm not sure there was any difference."

"There is a huge difference, Karen. Studying comes from the intellect but atonement comes from the heart. "

Werner, smiling smugly, says something in German and Karl translates, "He says that Marilyn is the holy mother of cataclysm and rectification."

Marilyn replies sternly to Werner in German.

"I won't translate that," Karl laughs.

"My husband is referring to the fact that after I visit these places full of death and suffering," Marilyn hesitates and lowers her eyes to the napkin she is fiddling with in her lap, "I visit a retreat, some spot of cleansing and renewal."

"What do you mean? What kind of places?" Karen can't imagine.

"Well, I took several weeks to walk the major part of the…um…" here she looks to Karl for help.

"Santiago de Compostela," he fills in the blank.

"Yes. And, I went to the River Jordan to be baptized and to walk the Stations of the Cross. I went to a temple in Tibet to chant with the monks." Werner motions to the waiter to take their order after which Marilyn continues, "I imagine I sound like some kind of nut." Werner nods his agreement, but Marilyn goes on un-phased. "Atonement. Who validates atonement? Nobody believes in God anymore, but I desperately believe that its critical we behave as though we do. Who is to forgive us if not God?" Marilyn seems to want an answer and not receiving one goes on, "America is filled with places where horrendous things have happened and yet, in order to neutralize those horrors, I had to leave America. America has no sacred places. Oh, it has churches, but it has no truly sacred places."

"It's true," Karen realizes. "I've been to St. Patrick's Cathedral in New York but that feels more like a business or a tourist attraction than a sacred place. France has Lourdes, Italy has the Vatican, Mexico has Our Lady of Guadalupe. America has Disneyland."

Everyone laughs except Karen. The table goes silent. Then, Karl, emptying his sake cup, says "Acts of unspeakable horror, acts of super-human charity, they both come from the same general impetus: Desire with a capital D: the desire, by some, to murder, but the desire not to be murdered: the desire to be forgiven, and the desire to grant forgiveness: the desire to love and be loved. And what is it that creates desire? One basic human instinct: passion. Whether it is cruelty or mercy, it gets us all riled, sets our passions burning. Perhaps America is on the right track with a passion to entertain and to be entertained. Disneyland is sort of anti-everything. The opposite of

Disneyland, the happiest place on Earth, is a place like Haiti, I suppose. The point is: what do we desire? How shall we channel our passions? That's the question. If we truly desire peace, why are we always at war? What passion are we satisfying? What do we truly desire?"

"Sex," says Werner in English and everyone laughs that, of all the English words Werner knows, this is the most intelligible.

That seems to change the mood of the conversation, lighten it. Dinner comes and the table quiets for a while before the conversation begins again. The meal is finished. The plates are cleared and coffee is served.

"We're going on to Tsubaki for Misogi," Marilyn says dabbing at her mouth and then tossing her napkin on the table. "You should come with us."

"Mi…? What? What's that?"

"Misogi is a purification ritual…washing away one's sins. No, not sins, washing away one's misery."

Karen finds herself enthusiastically agreeing.

The next morning Karen has second thoughts. She had planned to spend two more days in Hiroshima before returning to Tokyo for her flight home. She owes it to her father to be the witness he wanted her to be. Still, the notion of balancing something like the Hiroshima experience with a Shinto ritual of purification appeals to Karen. The four of them agreed to meet in the lobby after breakfast to arrange for a bus to take them on to Tsubaki. Karen packs her bags and meets them at the appointed time.

III

Marilyn's greeting assures Karen that she is risking nothing by changing her plans, assures Karen that, in fact, this is the path her father would have taken. The four travelers board a bus that will take them to Tsubaki. Werner and Karl sit in a seat in front of Marilyn and Karen. For three hours, the bus winds its way through narrow, tree-lined roads and small villages before it climbs into a mountainous region and, forty-five minutes later, stops in front of the entrance to the shrine. No cars are allowed inside the gate and they stand in the road with their luggage spread around them. The Germans have enormous backpacks and Marilyn carries a small cosmetics case in addition. Karen, on the other hand, has a large roller bag and struggles with a carry-on she's stuffed with snacks, books, toothbrush and toothpaste and anything else she thought she might need if her luggage were lost. Inside the shrine gates, they have to carry their luggage themselves.

Beyond the torii gate, a cobblestone path lined with flower beds and pine forests lead to a welcome center, in front of which stands a priest clad in a white and blue kimono. The noise of the wheels of Karen's roller bag thunder along the cobblestones in the otherwise peaceful setting until Karl and Werner swoop from behind to pick up the bag, laughing good-naturedly, and restoring the path to its meditative peacefulness. As they approach the priest, he welcomes them with a deep bow and a greeting in English; he leads them along the path chatting casually, drawing attention to small statues of Buddha that mark the path, to the sounds of birds, to the azaleas in bloom, until they reach a dark wooden, one-story inn where they will sleep. Removing their shoes and sliding into the slippers provided, they enter a room covered in golden-brown tatami mats with a stack of once-colorful futons in the corner. The room is scattered with black lacquer trays on legs that raise the tray several inches for eating; visitors sit on red cushions drinking tea or playing a game with stones on a board. "Goh," the priest smiles and nods at the players. "Very famous Japanese game."

Many people are clad in the cotton, summer kimono the priest calls yakata. They lounge on the thick mats and talk or play at the low tables. Toward the back of the room, luggage is stacked. The men add the group's luggage to the pile.

The priest shows them where they can get a yakata and towel, and leads them to the entrance of the bath. "Please stroll the grounds, enjoy a bath, but return for dinner at eight o'clock." The priest readies to leave them. "After dinner we will begin the lessons."

It is late afternoon before they begin walking the grounds. Marilyn becomes quieter, withdrawn. She lags behind the others, slowing her pace, stopping to make notes in her journal, looking down at her feet as if each step must be thought out carefully. The men seem to be amused by Marilyn and speak about her in German without translating. Soon, Karen finds herself falling into Marilyn's meditative mood, separating herself from her traveling companions, following a different path, stopping to regard a particular flower or leaf.

Off the main path of the shrine grounds, down a narrower, dirt trail, Karen is drawn by a huge tree with a belt of rope and paper that surrounds the tree about four feet from the ground. Karen is not in Christian territory. She is in a Shinto shrine where all of nature is the physical manifestation of God. She stretches out her hand to touch the tree's bark, then sits down under the tree as though instructed and rests her back against its trunk. The contact is enormously comforting. The smell of the cool earth and flowers, the softness of the decomposing bark on which she sits, the mystic colors that dance before her eyes when she closes them, so comforting, all so comforting. But soon she stirs at the voices of children come to lay their hands on the tree. "Konichi-wa," Karen greets the two little boys as she gets up, but the children only stare at the tall, pale woman, their eyes following her as she walks away.

Karen slowly makes her way back to the communal sleeping room. When she doesn't see Marilyn, Werner, or Karl, she pulls out a mat to lie down. She feels suddenly spent, exhausted as if she could sleep for days. Her eyes are closed, but she doesn't sleep. Across her eyelids are visions of a little Japanese boy on his way to school, his laces untied, his expression bored pondering the prospect of another school day. Then, the little boy transforms into her brother, Kyle; her father appears and Kyle takes his father's hand, shepherding him safely to some final destination. The sound of mats being laid down with a gentle smack rouse Karen from her dreams; She hears the pieces slide across the goh board and people softly snoring or chatting. She smells the pungent odor of cigarette smoke. Sometime later, Karl, and Werner return from their walk; a little after them, Marilyn returns. Marilyn softly shakes Karen's shoulder. "Let's go to the bath," she says.

They pick up a small towel and a bar of soap and head into the women's section of the bath. Undressing, they fold their clothes and place them, along with their yakatas, in a basket to store on a shelf. Karen had almost forgotten the scars left on her body from the accident that killed Gary. The doctors had taken half her stomach and removed ruptured ovaries where the steering wheel had cut into her. Circular scars mark the spots where there were pins to hold her right leg together while it healed and a long, thin scar runs almost the entire length of her shin. The scars have long ago lost their redness but suddenly they seem more visible in front of Marilyn. No one but a handful of doctors had seen her naked body since Gary's death. But Marilyn either doesn't see Karen's scarred body or sees without reaction. They follow the example of the other bathers and wash by sitting on low stools, soaping up, and pouring washbasins of water over themselves, then move through frosted glass doors to the outside natural hot springs. A thick wisteria trellis shades one of the pools; another pool flows back into a grotto sparkling with blue lights. Women lounge on boulders of various sizes that surround each pool or sink themselves up to their necks in the steaming water.

Without speaking, Marilyn and Karen go their separate ways. Rocks form borders and platforms for each pool and Karen sits on a rock then slips down into the pool. The water is amazingly soft and fragrant—not sulphur springs but true mineral springs. Her shoulders loosen, a sigh of sheer pleasure escapes from her as she relaxes. It all seems gloriously unfamiliar here at a Shinto shrine tucked into the mountains of Japan, and it doesn't take long for Karen to totally lose awareness of Marilyn. Climbing out of the pool and stretching herself out on a rock to let the sun warm her, something in her lifts.

The priest said something earlier that day as he ushered their small group from the shrine gates to the guesthouse; he stopped to point out the beauty of the camellias. "We say mono-no-aware." The priest pronounced "aware" like "a-war-ray" reminding her of her father's lesson on the subject. "This word" the priest continued, "expresses the transience of all living things." The priest nodded his head, beckoning them with his eyes to come enjoy the camellias. "Mono-no-aware" he continued in his stiff, formal English, "tells us to observe these camellias and appreciate them so that when they are gone, we will remember them with loving fondness, not with sadness. We will understand that it's the natural cycle of life and we will be heartened by the knowledge that the camellias will return in the spring." He smiled and bobbed his head up and down encouraging their small party to observe and move on.

Sunning herself, Karen realizes that she wasn't consciously thinking about Gary's death when the priest explained mono-no-aware, but thinking about it now, she sits up on the rock. Gary died a long time ago. Karen had spent two years recovering from the accident... or recovering from the broken leg, the internal injuries that left her unable to have children. Her bones mended but emotional and psychological recovery was impossible. After a decade though, Karen settled into a life that went on almost normally. All the deaths seem to meld into one, her brother's while she was still in high school, her mother's when Karen was in her late twenties, then, her husband, and now her father. Still, some weight has lifted.

"Are you ready? Shall we scrub?" Marilyn is suddenly standing beside her. Karen is not ready, but she gets up and follows Marilyn back to the wash room to do their final scrub, then to the dressing room.

They return to the common room in their yakatas, hair still gleaming wet with the mineral water, to low black lacquer trays being set up in long rows; a red cushion is placed behind each tray.

Karl looks up at them. "The baths must agree with you," he says, not clearly addressing one or the other. "You're glowing!" He moves a goh piece and says, "They're just bringing out some tea. And, a priest passed out the pamphlets." He hands one to Karen and one to his sister.

"Are there any in German?" Marilyn frowns.

"There were some, but I think they're all taken. English is the best I can do."

Karen takes the brochure and sits with her back against the wall. Marilyn retrieves her notebook and pen, pulls out a futon and folding it into a mound, rests on her elbow.

After a while, the men get up and go outside. A few minutes later, Marilyn gets up too.

"Karen," she says, "they're lighting the fire. Don't you want to come and see?"

The clatter of dishes from the kitchen indicates that dinner will soon be served. Karen feels lazy, not so much tired, as lethargic. She'd just as soon stay where she is, but she gathers her strength, pulls herself up, and follows Marilyn through the shoji screens, along the veranda, and down a path bordered with azaleas. The sun has disappeared behind the mountains. The group, primarily Japanese but with a few Westerners, has gathered. Werner raises a hand to signal their location and the two women settle into spots beside the men just as the priest touches the torch to the wood. Most of the pilgrims, including the four of them, are still in thin cotton yakatas. The air has turned cold. They huddle together to warm themselves. When the fire catches, the chill disappears. Karl and Werner joke that the ritual they will learn is nothing more than American football. Marilyn ignores them, sitting pensively, her blue eyes on the fire. It is completely dark now; the mountain air begins to be uncomfortably cold, but soon the priest shoos the group in for dinner.

All tolled, in the English language section, there are no more than a dozen participants whom the priest refers to as penitents or pilgrims, along with three priests. One of the priests speaks briefly, then a dinner of rice, mountain vegetables, and green tea is served. When everyone is finished eating, the trays are removed and the instruction begins.

When the priest begins the instruction, his English is not nearly as good as the priest who had introduced them to the shrine. They catch a word here and there but much of the priest's explanation is lost. Karen soon begins to get the rhythm of his speech and understands a little better as the priest tells the story of standing under the waterfall every midnight for an initial period of ten years. He did this as a spiritual exercise to calm and nourish his own soul. He spoke of miracles that blessed him because of his spiritual purity and Karl chuckles a little and Marilyn jabs an elbow into Karl's side and hisses something at him. Then, exasperated, she turns to Karen, "The whole point is to take a moment for introspection." Marilyn turns to frown at Karl then back to Karen. "The whole point is to examine one's soul."

After a while, Karen glances toward Marilyn, who has fallen into a state that can only be described as mesmerized. The priest tells the penitents that they have been prepared by avoiding meat, alcohol, and caffeine at dinner and he hopes that they have prepared themselves by avoiding sexual contact. Karl mutters something to Werner who laughs but Marilyn is too intent to reprimand them.

The ritual movements, clapping, thrusting forward, feinting back, are intended to focus the penitent, move the attention from the mind to the body; the shouting of syllables sync the brain to the movements. The quartet gets it wrong, trying again and again. It is the Yielding sequence that captures Karen the most. In Yielding, the pilgrims stand with their legs slightly apart for steadiness and place their left hand on their hip. With a gesture not unlike a Boy Scout salute, the members of the group extend their right hand with two fingers straight but with the other fingers curled; then, making a sweeping gesture with their right hand cutting through the air, they shout Japanese syllables, the meaning of which is forgotten in the struggle to replicate the sound.

"We will complete these exercises facing the waterfall," the priest tells them. "Then, one by one, you will be sprinkled with salt and take your turn under this god in the form of falling water in the ritual called Misogi Harae."

The priest hands each penitent a red and white hachimaki or headband that he says with a broad smile is a "graduation present." Marilyn helps Karen tie the hachimaki around her head and then Karen helps Marilyn. "A hachimaki helps the wearer persevere," the priest says, "and have courage. Warriors wear hachimaki to strengthen their spirits." Then, the priest leads them single file from the room.

Several more fires have been lit bathing the night in golden light and warming the air. When the group comes in sight of the waterfall, the half-dozen priests stop the pilgrims to lead them through the ritual. Karen performs with strict concentration and is even a little proud. Then the group continues down the path halting at three stone steps that lead down to a ledge. The priests position themselves along the route to the waterfall.

The women go first, being helped into the water and then out again, their hair dripping and their yakatas clinging. They are, one by one, wrapped in a blanket and then directed to follow the path to the fires where they sit on logs warming themselves. A wooden box of hot, sweet, milky, sake awaits them.

Karen's turn will come right after Marilyn. Even as she watches, Marilyn seems transformed. As Marilyn waits before the waterfall, the priest sprinkles a pinch of salt over her. Facing the waterfall, Marilyn bows twice, claps twice, bows once more, then slices the air across her body. "Yei!" Marilyn calls out. Her eyes are closed, her hands in the gesture of prayer. Her body is stiff when the priests tilt her into the waterfall, but when she emerges, her body is limp. There is peacefulness in Marilyn's expression, in her posture. She repeats the bowing and clapping and reaches for the blanket the priest wraps around her. She makes her way down the path.

Karen takes her turn, executing the ritual, stepping up carefully. She stretches out her hand to meet the outstretched hand of the priest. The clapping, the salt, the blessing, then turning, falling back, then under the waterfall. It's seconds really, but something happens. This water rushing over her (this comes to her not as thought but as experience) is eternal, endless and, for that moment, she is one with it—eternal as the water.

Moments later, Karen sits placidly next to Marilyn, their bodies touching, holding their wooden sake boxes in both hands. Karen wants to ask Marilyn about her experience, but neither of them can speak of it; not yet. They watch as first Werner and then Karl perform the purification rite; then, the men join them by the fire. Both men seem oddly sobered by the experience. The wisecracks give way to silence.

People converse in whispers; then, slowly, everyone drifts back to the common sleeping room. Karen is exhausted. She changes into dry clothes, spreads her futon, covers herself with a quilt, and goes to sleep immediately. When she awakes, Marilyn, Karl, and Werner are still sleeping. Most people are already up, making their way to the bathrooms carrying their grooming kits. Some have already taken up their futons and have moved to the side of the room where kettles of tea sit on burners. Karen takes a cup of tea and goes outside to get a last glimpse of the waterfall. When the bells ring for breakfast, Werner, Karl, and Marilyn are dressed and packed and are sitting on their red cushions drinking tea and eating their morning rice. Karen picks up a bowl of rice, chopsticks, and a fresh cup of tea and sits down on the cushion they have saved for her.

"Looks like this is it," Karl looks at Karen and sighs. "By Monday it will be back to the old grind."

The old grind, Karen thinks. If only. She is facing a brand new grind, as familiar as the old one maybe but exponentially more difficult. Her father's clothes still hang in his closet, his shaving brush and mug is still in the bathroom, his shoes are still by the door. The bed where he drew his last breath has been stripped of its sheets but the mattress still bears the stains of his body's released fluids. Still grinding, yes, but something entirely different. Karen smiles back at Karl. It hardly seems that they'd known each other less than two full days.

"Thanks for rescuing me," Karen says, as much to Marilyn as to Karl.

"Did we rescue you?" Karl asks.

"In the coffee shop? You wondered if I was okay?"

"And are you okay?" The question seems genuine. Karl's eyes are square on Karen's, embarrassing her in front of Marilyn and Werner.

"I didn't tell you that, less than a month ago, my father passed away. Going home again will seem...well...odd, I guess...with him not there. He and I had lived together for twenty years...since my mother died. He was the last of my family."

Marilyn immediately takes Karen's hand, "I'm so sorry! We didn't know!"

"So you all rescued me," she tells them, looking at Marilyn who is still holding her hand.

Marilyn records Karen's name, address, telephone number, and email address in her notebook and tears out a page with her information on it handing it to Karen. Karl adds his email address to the page.

"Germany is a wonderful country—you should come visit. We live just southwest of Hamburg almost to Bremen." Karl is no longer looking at Karen, making her feel that Karl's invitation is insincere, just something people say.

"I'd like that." Karen is being polite right back.

"When can you come?" Marilyn has her pen and paper out and is ready to write down the dates of Karen's arrival and this makes Karen laugh.

"I don't know!" Karen's voice falters; the amusement of a minute ago is gone as suddenly as it came. " I have a lot of things to settle with my father's estate." That is half a lie. There are no heirs except Karen. Her father's shoes can stay by the door for decades if she chooses.

Werner looks at his watch and says something in German. Karl, Werner, and Marilyn stand. It's time for their bus. They will leave from Kansai airport in Osaka while Karen needs to return to Tokyo for a flight from Narita. Her bus isn't for another hour. Marilyn gives Karen a long, lingering hug; Karen waves to them until their bus is out of sight. An hour later, she boards a bus as well, settling in a seat by a window.

She feels lucky. The company was welcome. Meeting with Karl, traveling with him, his sister, and his brother-in-law, was like having a context again, like meeting long lost cousins for the first time. Or like a convention of some bizarre club, some gathering of survivors intent on comforting one another.

After her mother died, her father wandered angrily around the backyard, his hands clenching into fists, then unclenching over and over until finally he'd fall to his knees and call out to his lost wife as though he could summon her home, as though his grief could restore his wife to him so that when he lifted his head he would see her walking through the backyard gate. Karen watched him from the kitchen window and wept, thinking her father would go mad or that she would go mad watching him. Then, one spring he planted a flowering cherry tree and every year he would look forward to the tree's blossoms. His grief seemed no longer crushing. When the last bloom vanished from the tree, he would simply sigh and say that everything is allotted its time.

Karen transfers from the bus to the train that will take her to Narita. The Japanese landscape disappears behind her as she looks ahead, watching for the next village, the next train station, everything come and gone in a second. She presses her forehead against the cold glass of the train window thinking of her father's cherry tree in the backyard and feeling the weight of Karl's email address in her pocket.

Home

Maxine's mother had bartered some jewelry...a diamond brooch and perhaps some rings...for the house between the railroad tracks and the river on the edge of Stringtown. Thegri Turgovian McGuire seemed to know about houses like this and about men like Thom Sloane, the real estate broker, who she knew would consider the house a blemish on the pillar of his otherwise well-painted reputation. In fact, after strolling the prosperous lanes that fanned out from the town square like sunbeams, Thegri figured the town was already putting pressure on Mr. Sloane to tear down the house and that he would happily accept anything at all for it, the real price being the transfer of responsibility for the place. Maxine knew the house wouldn't change much just because the McGuire family moved into it. It had been a railroad hotel and a brothel and she knew the chipped paint and the sagging back porch which gave it the forlorn look of the abandoned would not change with her mother's heavy brocade drapes. Still, this was the right house for them. Somehow it was fitting. There were stories about that house, random stories that didn't really make a coherent history, and there were stories about the McGuires too. Stories about Thegri McGuire always seemed to go around and come around transformed like cream in a butter churn. Later, for instance, when Thom Sloane would talk about selling the house to her, he'd say it was the time he had been bewitched. Maxine was used to it. She could almost anticipate Mr. Sloane's tone, like the teller was spinning a yarn or telling a ghost story. And she could predict key words, too, stressed and repeated like a chant: how they'd say that her mother had a "haunting" look or how she'd "hypnotized" or "tricked" them. It was true. Her mother had eyes set deep in dark round hollows like black rocks half-exposed in muddy water and dark hair that stood electrified around her small face. Still, she was very beautiful with her dark, untroubled skin and the calm way she had. She'd taught Mickey and Maxine to listen and to observe. The three of them used to walk to the grocery in town...the two children following behind their mother's long swinging strides...each carrying a basket, and they'd listen to the strangers' talk. It was common for Mickey and Maxine to hear their mother referred to as "that McGuire woman" or "that gypsy."

  Mickey understood that their mother was a foreigner despite the fact that she'd been born in New Jersey. She was like someone medieval he said and she knew less about the world than he knew in some ways; she could tell almost anything about an individual but society collectively was a mystery. Mickey already knew, for instance, that the McGuires would never be part of any community in Stringtown anymore than they had been anywhere else. The sad part was that Thegri Turgovian wanted so badly for her children to belong in a way that Mickey and Maxine figured they never would.

  If you walked along the railroad tracks from their house and then turned toward the town square, Stringtown Elementary School was right there, between their house and town. Maxine knew the minute she saw it that things were going to be different from here on out; not that the school *looked* all that different from the schools in Sioux Falls, Tulsa, or Cleveland, but that it *felt* different. Her mother had promised that this place, this town, would be different and Maxine believed her mother really *knew* it in the same way she knew about Thom Sloane. Stringtown was small and they would have friends she said and they'd live in a house, just their family. No cousins, no aunts. Just her, Mickey and Maxine. This time Maxine and Mickey could finish out the entire year in a single school.

By the end of summer, the whole town knew the McGuires; Thegri with her educated, foreign way of speaking and her two dark children, Mickey and Maxine, always trailing behind her. Mickey at sixteen was already as tall as a man and as broad shouldered. Both children were olive-skinned but Mickey had green eyes the color of the curative waters kept in vials on his mother's shelf. He was dark and silent and sulky.

Maxine was tall and as thin as pulled taffy as her Uncle Cae used to say. Her eyes were grey and she sometimes thought of them as one-way mirrors.

It was possible during the summer months for them to keep pretty much to themselves; they could pull themselves back, contain themselves in the quarter-acre of land that they knew to be their friendly world. But then school started and there Mickey and Maxine were as odd as sparrows in a robin's nest.

But the way Maxine saw it, some things were different already. For the first time, she and Mickey had new clothes bought especially for the first day of school; Mickey had a new pair of blue jeans and a white t-shirt and Maxine had a red and blue plaid dress with a belt that buckled around the waist. None of them had more than sturdy worn-out shoes. Her mother had washed and braided Maxine's hair as though the act itself were a ritual, one that insured Maxine's acceptance. Mickey walked with his sister as far as the elementary school and then walked on by himself to Grover Cleveland High School in town. After school, he would wait for Maxine at the gate so that he could walk her home again.

Mickey walked silently, unsmiling. Maxine was proud of him and she loved him but his fierce defensiveness almost shamed her. He looked wary as if every corner presented possibility for ambush. And he held his chin out and his shoulders back as though there were already something or someone to defy. She could feel his dread of another school, another group of strangers who would form opinions of him, his sister, and their mother. Maxine knew Mickey only meant to protect her, to shield her, but she also knew that's what made him such an easy target. So she walked beside him or a little behind until they got to the school where his green eyes would follow her until she was safe inside with the school doors closed behind her.

She had always managed to do well in school but Mickey was lucky to be in high school at all. The adjustments to the varieties of teachers, schools, and towns seemed to urge Maxine to be more adaptable while Mickey just sunk lower and lower trying to second guess what was expected of him by this teacher, in this school, in this town. While Mickey used up all his energy keeping the world at bay, Maxine used hers to absorb it, to become part of it in the way that the roads on the edge of town were part of it. While Mickey worked to preserve his identity, Maxine worked to dissolve hers. All Mickey wanted was to get out of Stringtown and all Maxine wanted was to make it home.

Mickey did get out, at least temporarily. Every time Mickey hopped the train that passed by their house, Maxine held her breath. She sat on the back stoop watching the hard, fast steel wheels of the train and watching Mickey, his eyes fastened on the open door of a car, position himself to lunge forward and throw himself up and in. He rode the train the twenty miles to Ellsinore. When it came down to it, Mickey looked more like his Irish father than his Romanian mother and he could pass for eighteen in almost any bar to get himself a three-two beer. Maxine knew where he was off to even if her mother didn't. Mickey was off to Tiny's. It was down a dirt road next to a small sawmill where the sawmill workers would come in after work for a beer before they went home. On Saturdays, Tiny's served chicken fried steak or catfish. Whoever ate out in Ellsinore ate at Tiny's. The jukebox would swallow one dime after another and husbands danced with wives, holding infants between them as they swirled around the dance floor.

  At first Mickey went there just to get out of Stringtown on a Saturday night but soon he went to watch Mona wait tables. She was plain at first glance, but the more Mickey looked at her the more her plainness vanished. It was her hips mainly that attracted him. She slithered and weaved around the tables swiveling her hips to keep the big round tray level as she balanced it on one strong arm over her head. She noticed him too. He'd sit nursing his draft beer 'til it was warm and flat all the while keeping his eyes on Mona's comings and goings. On slow nights, Mona'd stand in the doorway that led to the kitchen and smoke a cigarette while she stared back at him.

  She was older, Mickey knew it. And she'd been married once and had a couple of kids. Mickey thought someday he would dance with her and they could hold one of her babies between them just like the other couples on the dance floor. Stringtown girls shunned the gypsy Mickey McGuire, but here in Tiny's, Mickey McGuire was just a brawny young Irishman come to drink a beer and flirt with Mona.

There was no way for Mickey to know that Mona's husband wasn't gone for good, or that, paralyzed and in a wheel chair, he'd level his rifle through the bedroom window and tear a furrow across Mickey's behind deep enough to plant petunias in. But the incident didn't phase Mickey; it only gave him a taste of what a woman could be like when he sank deep into her like she was a deep-dish apple pie.

After that, Mickey went one town further to Crockett and then one town further 'til he went so far he couldn't come and go in one day's time anymore and it took the whole of a weekend. His mother would stand at the back window, waiting for the next train to come by, waiting to see the form of her young man jump from an empty car as it sped past, and then roll in quick, painful summersaults almost to their doorstep.

At night Maxine slept in her room, content that her mother had kept her promise, while her mother stood at the back door waiting for Mickey to come home. Maxine didn't understand why she worried; Mickey was nearly a man.

Summer passed without incident but towards the start of the next school year, Mickey seemed moody. Her mother, half with love and half with accusation, said he was like his father, temperamental and morose. His green eyes flashed. He was proud to be like his father.

Thegri insisted that Mickey continue to walk Maxine to school even though Maxine was in the seventh grade and almost a teenager herself. They seldom spoke as they walked anymore. She could sense an easier presence beside her. His mind was somewhere out of Stringtown with buxom women and flat beer while Maxine's mind was on *Tale of Two Cities* or *Huckleberry Finn*. Still, every morning as he left her at the elementary school gate, he kissed her forehead and every afternoon her heart jumped as she saw her handsome brother strutting toward her.

It was late fall when Mickey left. He simply left Maxine waiting at the schoolyard gate. She waited an hour and then, from the direction of the house, her mother came. There was always something portentous in unexpectedly seeing Thegri Turgovian. Her long strides brought her closer and closer, her skirt swirling around her legs as she walked, her shawl held tightly around her, clasped by both fists to her chest. She was like a prophet come out of the woods, someone Biblical and holy. She was like a ghost made flesh or a cat transfigured.

Maxine waited at the gate until her mother reached her, and then, without words, Maxine followed her mother home.

Fear, not patience, kept Maxine from asking where Mickey had gone. She was afraid he might be dead, the victim of some amorous accident, or that he might be in prison. Everyday, her mother walked her to school and her mother was there waiting at the gate when Maxine came out again.

Thegri began sleeping on a cot downstairs in the kitchen so she could hear the trains and the turn of the back door knob. Her bedroom door remained closed and her bedroom unoccupied. Two months passed before Maxine got up the courage to ask. Her mother was in the kitchen tearing bread to make bread pudding.

"Mother." She was always silent but Maxine knew she had her attention. "When is Mickey coming home again?"

"I don't know."

"Where is he?"

"I don't know," she said, "He left with his father."

"Mr. McGuire came to get Mickey?" Maxine had the habit of calling him formally because she never remembered seeing him herself and she'd only heard him referred to by people who called on the phone or came to the door to ask for him.

"Yes," she said, "but he won't get you. Mickey wanted to go. When his father came, Mickey was ready."

Mickey had been four years old when Thegri left Mr. McGuire behind and Maxine was still a week from being born. She went first to her mother's for Maxine's birth, then on to cousins, brothers, aunts and friends in a string of migrations that lead forward and back but never anyplace called home. There were places of their own on occasion and Thegri's romances that sometimes promised to be permanent but never were.

Life went on, of course, even after Mickey had gone. Thegri continued to earn a few dollars selling homemade cold remedies and plasters, selling fresh and dried herbs, mushrooms and fruits and vegetables she'd canned. Every now and then a stranger, or someone vaguely familiar from town would be at their back door. On the sly, wary and ducking, they'd ask Thegri for a sumbul root or a love potion and give her a few dollars. A necklace would be sold or a gold bracelet. Part of her inheritance she said. Money would come to her in the mail. They got by.

One day, when Maxine and her mother got home from school, there was Mickey, sitting on the back porch stoop wearing an Army uniform. It hadn't worked out like he'd thought, he said. He thought his father was the high rolling bar brawler and ladies man his mother had always made him out to be. He thought he and his father would have good times romancing the ladies in the flowered sheets of their own beds and drinking whiskey from bottles clothed in brown paper. But Michael McGuire was just an run of the mill married man trying, like Stringtown men, to make a living for his family. His father's red-haired second wife had a temper to keep pace with her husband's. He had three little girls with the new Mrs. McGuire and all he wanted was to train Mickey to help out in the car repair shop he'd built up. He would train him so he could make a good living. This wasn't what Mickey had in mind at all. Mr. McGuire had fixed Mickey a place in a room he'd built over the shop and they'd work together in the garage, the father teaching his son about engines and spark plugs and how to pull the dent out of a car until nightfall, when greasy and tired, the other Mrs. McGuire put the green beans and ham on the table. Mickey felt stuck in the same dead end he was stuck in in Stringtown.

But he'd made a friend. Matt hung around the garage and was going to join the Army when he graduated. Only Matt decided not to wait because he was flunking out of school anyway so they both joined the Army together and Mickey was just in Stringtown to say goodbye before he went back to Fort Leonard Wood to finish basic training.

It was the first time any of the Turgovian family had ever been in the service of any kind in any country. His mother touched his shorn head, straightened his tie, and shined his belt buckle with the hem of her skirt and never once stopped touching him. Even as he sat down to eat, her hand was on his knee. Maxine could hardly recognize Mickey in all of this. These crisp clothes that made him look like discipline personified, and money in his pocket for the first time ever. He had a whole new confidence. Before he left he hugged and kissed Maxine and promised his mother he would write and send money too.

They went to stand next to the highway to flag down the Greyhound bus. Even as he climbed the stairs of the bus, his mother's hand touched the heel of his shiny black shoe as if she knew this goodbye would have to last a long, long time.

Years after that, after Thegri Turgovian McGuire had died, a letter arrived for her from the Department of State.

Home 145

If Stringtown hadn't been so small the post office would have returned the letter to the sender addressee unknown, but the postmaster knew that the sole surviving member of the McGuire family was Maxine McGuire Huffy. Because mail wasn't delivered out on the ridge, the postmaster had the entire day to glimpse the official looking letter in their mail slot before Sonny came to pick it up and bring it home.

Mickey'd been missing in action in Viet Nam for twenty-three years now. No death benefits (a term Maxine's mother had puzzled over for a long while before asking Maxine to explain) and no American flag folded into a triangle like a puffy red, white, and blue tart were due an M.I.A. It would be seven years after he was declared missing, seven years to the day, that Mickey would be legally dead. Even then, there could be no funeral. There was no body and no grave either; the Army explained that legally dead and officially dead were two different things absolutely. Legally dead only meant that as far as the court was concerned a spouse was now a widow, etc. The McGuire family was assured that, Mickey might, in fact, be alive. Legally dead only released the death benefits and released the Army from monthly paychecks. So there were long nights in which Thegri Turgovian stood at the open back door, staring out at the railroad tracks waiting for the familiar thud and tumble of Mickey's body to roll from the train like a happy, drunken, legally dead mail sack.

When they were first notified that Mickey was missing, Thegri chanted for a hundred nights for the recovery of what had been lost. For hundreds more nights, potions were mixed and burned for the return of an errant loved one. Shreds of Mickey's old shirts, washed in lucky bluing and stuck to a wax doll rested on the kitchen sill like a miniature transparent corpse. But Mickey didn't come home. Every night Maxine fell asleep to the rhythms of her mother's chants drowned out only by the occasional grind and whoof of a passing train. Thegri seemed never to sleep in those days; if Maxine woke in mid-night she could hear the creaking boards testifying to her mother's vigil.

The Turgovian family, by whatever loose organization that family was defined, began to come and go. Sometimes Maxine would be roused from sleep by some stranger's voice, some relative, some friend come in the night to look into the face of Thegri Turgovian's offspring, and to offer a séance hoping to connect with some departed soul who might know if Mickey McGuire were among them; or perhaps they'd lend a special potion to aid Mickey's return and then they'd be gone leaving behind only stains on earnestly set tea cups. The visitors were quick to remind Thegri that Mickey had been dead the moment he had become one of them, one of those soldiers who represented allegiance to place and government. Soldiers with guns lost their cunning they told her. They lost the knack of surviving by their wits; they lost the necessity. They were merely targets for other witless soldiers with guns in an endless arcade game without winners, without prizes. At the moment that Mickey McGuire became willing to kill for an impersonal cause, he became pure Irish, one with his father's blood.

Since Mickey had left, Maxine had adjusted to being one of a kind. Neither fully part of Stringtown, nor part of any real family, giving up making sense of the past and struggling to define some kind of future, she emulated her friend Vicki English. In some ways, Mickey's absence had been a boon. The protection Mickey had provided, however well-intentioned, had also served as a barrier. When Maxine was free of his protective shield, she became free to expose herself fully to the town.

The comings and goings at the McGuire house lasted five years and ended near spring in 1967. A man came to the door. He was roundly fat with black shiny hair that Maxine could see his scalp through. He wore rings--two on one hand and three on the other--that cut into his fat fingers like wide gold strings tied around sausages. He leaned on a cane that bent in an arc under his weight. Her mother called him Poppy although Maxine was sure this man was not her mother's father; they walked together down by the river's edge.

After that, Thegri seemed herself again. She went back to sleeping in her bedroom; visitors no longer came and went in the dead of night; there were no potions, no wax dolls and no chants.

Thegri never explained to her daughter who the man was or what he'd said but Maxine knew that the man had brought her mother peace. It was as though the man had convinced Thegri that her son had happily passed. Perhaps he had even brought greetings to her from her son on the other side. In death, Mickey McGuire had come home again. Even Maxine felt comforted. It was as if, while he was alive, his spirit was not free to roam and visit because it was locked inside his living body. Once departed, thus free of the body, Thegri might see him down by the river and carry on a conversation, get the news. Thegri felt contented. And so did Maxine. At least she had her mother back again. Everything was on the same shifting and ethereal plane Maxine was used to.

When Thegri Turgovian McGuire died, Sonny gathered her possessions and brought them to his wife. He brought the shoe box with Mickey's paychecks; he brought the manuals and the cakes of paraffin and the sumbul root. He brought the long patterned skirts that she had stored in trunks, wearing only blue jeans and cotton shirts as a compromise with Maxine. It really wasn't much. No family albums. No insurance policies. Thegri had converted most of the jewelry and odds and ends of leather, silk and fur to cash years before and even opened a regular bank account at Maxine's insistence. There was a small wooden chest, though, that held a picture of Mickey in his Army uniform and some letters he had written. A few loose stones rattled around in the bottom of the box and there was a ring that had belonged to Mr. McGuire. Nothing really.

When the letter came, addressed to Mrs. Thegri McGuire and on official Department of State stationery, Maxine was momentarily stumped. Sonny brought it home to her and she stood it on the sideboard until they'd had dinner. It wasn't that she was intimidated or that she wanted to appear aloof, it was just that, at this late date, she felt sure that whatever news the Army had couldn't be very important. After dinner, Sonny and Maxine took the letter and sat on the couch. After cutting through the hem and haw of Army language, the letter said that some remains had been found that could all but be positively identified as those of Private Michael Ryan McGuire. The location of discovery was right, the proportion of the bones was right for someone his height, and other identifying techniques used by the team of Army coroners had borne out the probability that, at one time, these bones had held the flesh and heart of Private McGuire. Identifications in which neither teeth nor dog tags were found were never officially designated as positive identifications, but the Army, to the best of their expert knowledge and ability, had more or less determined that the bones were those of Maxine's brother. The remains would be arriving in a week's time by special mail.

As she held the letter in front of her, she didn't know whether to laugh or cry. It was absurd of the Army to suggest that she should be pleased or touched by the return of some random bones recovered from the jungles of Viet Nam, bones that may or may not be those of her brother. He had been lost for twenty years and more. It had been dealt with. Sorrow and grief had dribbled out like drops of blood from a small but painful cut. There was no emotional rush; none of the renting and tearing of garments that was the customary expression of grief in the Turgovian family. There was only slowly dying hope; only uncertainty that never quite vanished; only sounds in the night like Mickey stamping the dust off his boots before he came in the house or dark-haired, green-eyed strangers that were scrutinized across drugstore counters. But there was never again Mickey's face and never again Mickey's voice.

Sonny sat quietly looking down into the folded hands in his lap. "Do you think we should get a cemetery plot?" he said. He took Maxine's hand to bring her back from wherever he thought her mind had traveled. "Do you think we should buy a cemetery plot?" he repeated.

"Well," Maxine started but her thoughts were so deep within her that no other words formulated and surfaced. Sonny and Maxine had buried Thegri Turgovian McGuire in the town cemetery. At last Maxine had achieved a short history of place. Roots. But after a month, her mother's coffin had been dug up and only the stone remained before an empty hole. The Turgovian family had reclaimed their own. They'd taken her home, whoever they were and wherever home was. Maxine didn't yet know if she was willing to try again.

Days later the cardboard box arrived; not like a coffin, the box, but like the one that Mrs. English had brought Vicki's blue prom dress in. Mickey's box sat on the kitchen table through the night while Maxine rocked in the deck swing and looked out at the hills of Red Angel Ridge.

Maxine had abandoned her family and she knew it. She had been too anxious to convert them to up-right Stringtown citizens. She dressed her mother in jeans and western shirts, combed her hair into a neat bun, and dragged her into Citizen's National Bank to open an account as though that were the real test of one's legitimate existence, one's connection with real society and place. Now, all that seemed superficial. A loss. A mistake. She had abandoned them all right, and she had abandoned herself as well. As children, she and Mickey used to hang a bed sheet and gathering all the lamps and placing them behind, they would take turns making their dark anonymous shadows dance. There, dancing again, was her featureless shadow.

What sat on the kitchen table in the box was like a last testament; a will written in a language she could not understand enough even to ponder. Sitting at the kitchen table now with her hand resting on the box as though she might "hear" some message in the vibrations the box might give off, she wondered if she should look at the bones. Perhaps some message would reveal itself in the configuration; they would be cast like her mother had cast her yarrow sticks. Perhaps the uneven color or shading of the bones would spell out, would display...something...much like tracing faces in clouds. Perhaps Mickey would speak to her, forgive her for needing what she needed, and tell her what she should do with his bones.

As she sat, hand resting on the grey cardboard coffin, she felt moved to reach out to her mother as well, to complete the circle the three of them had made, to reunite them in some way. The gold loop earrings Maxine always wore were the ones taken from her mother's body. Her mother had worn the earrings as long as Maxine could remember. Now, Maxine wore them. Reaching up, she unfastened the loops and, opening Mickey's coffin, flung the earrings in. It was a motion she'd seen used a thousand times; the quick snap of her mother's wrist as she consummated a deal with the spirit world, flinging her potion into a blazing fire. Had the earth moved at the moment the golden rings met her brother's bones? A small earthquake? A mudslide? Had the house shifted on its spindly crutches? Was a storm rising? Was it simply the power of the moment and her own imagination?

Maxine reeled backwards feeling an airless shroud, like motion sickness, descend and cover her. She felt stricken as though, unwittingly, she'd performed one of her mother's ancient rituals. The medium at an uncomfortable séance, she felt taken over and manipulated. She saw herself as the near dead see themselves, from somewhere outside their own bodies.

When Sonny came home from the feed store, Maxine was still sitting in the swing on the deck. The sun was setting behind the red hills and the air smelled sweet with honeysuckle. Maxine was wrapped in the presence of her family's love. The unintended ritual had incorporated her mother's and brother's spirits into her own physical living body. She felt their weight and presence as surely as she felt her lungs breathing air. They were housed in her; joined in her until she joined with them.

Sonny served as the single pall bearer that moved Mickey's cardboard coffin from its resting place on the kitchen table, to its burial ground in the hall closet.

The Country of Her Most Beloved

My father left us during the hottest summer on record and the air conditioner, as though itself overwhelmed with misery, gave up its cooling ghost too. It wheezed and clunked and expired in the middle of a blazing day that must have been a hundred and five degrees. If those days were unbearable, the nights were killing. The usually cool nighttime desert remained stagnantly hot. I watched my mother suffer: from the heat, from sleeplessness, from the poverty that had now turned desperate, but most of all from the grief of losing my father...grief expressed around her eyes in concentric circles and around her lips in dry rays. I would hear the door open and close behind her, rise up on one elbow as if I had thoughts of stopping her, but then fall into sleep again. I seldom heard her come home, but, in the morning, she was always there. I envisioned her going nowhere, walking slowly along the dark, hot, unpaved street of our neighborhood. Or maybe driving, her hair stirred by the breeze of the open window. All my visions were lonely and sad and made my mother look like the last woman on Earth.

One late night when no air moved, I got up from my bed, my thin cotton gown drenched with sweat, to find my mother sitting in the backyard swing. An oppressive haze covered the entire night sky so that there was no brightness from the moon, but only from a streetlight in front of our house that shed pale light into the backyard. My mother sat with her face half in shadow. Her bare foot touched the baked clay earth to set the swing in lazy motion. When I sat down next to her, the wood of the swing felt warm from the night heat.

We didn't talked about my father, but everything seemed changed with the death of this one man. Even who he was seemed changed. There was no way to speak of him truthfully. It was as though it were necessary to alter memory. I didn't know why that was true; it just was. I had been afraid of him, afraid of his frustrated anger. It didn't seem right to say I'd been afraid. And, I'd been ashamed too...of his accent, of his long black moustache, of his rough hands. I know with certainty that my father loved me, loved me sometimes harshly. I know with certainty that my father loved my mother, too, but I couldn't point to one piece of evidence to validate that certainty. It wasn't like TV love—he offered her no surprise bouquets, no unexpected chocolates, no time that he swept her from her work at the kitchen sink for a close dance. That my mother loved my father was easier to see.

Suddenly, my mother stopped the swing. "Get dressed," she said as though she'd just remembered something amazing that she'd forgotten until that moment, some reserve of joy and enthusiasm newly rediscovered.

It wasn't how I'd pictured her nighttime adventures: my mother drifting through some un-peopled landscape, some place desolate and lonely and vacuous. She drove the car past the unpainted fences, out to where there were sidewalks and pots of flowers hanging from lampposts, and pulled in to the parking lot of a twenty-four hour grocery store. We walked through doors that opened automatically as though some invisible doorman stood sentry even at this late hour. Both of us sighed audibly and smiled in happy relief at the coolness that engulfed us. And it was bright. Every light in the store was blazing. Workers were busy in every aisle restocking the shelves, singing to the rock and roll music that filled the store from every corner. I couldn't have named it then, of course, but now I realize that part of the thrill of it was the incredible abundance that made us feel part of something miraculous. Although my mother had stopped holding my hand years ago, she took my hand. A man passed us pulling an empty pastry and bread cart and she pulled me over to the aisle where the man had just unloaded his goods.

"Feel," she said. We touched the warm bread as though it were a brand new baby. Our faces were full of the awe of it. Store bread still warm from the baker! And there was more to be grateful for: an aisle of freezer cases as long as a city block stuffed with cartons of ice cream, banana and pineapple popsicles, and other aisles with dozens of kinds of cereals, soups, salad dressings, jars of jellies, cookies stacked yards long and shelves high. It was a kind of heaven. Such wealth. Such choice. A treasure house really. Still, my mother had saved the best for last. Slowing our pace, we rounded the last corner to come face to face with a space so full of fresh produce that it took our breath away. Bright orange carrots were laid in pristine rows, their tops spread luxuriously behind them like fairy's hair: deep purple eggplant reminiscent of Christmas ornaments. Red, yellow and green peppers like traffic lights. Pyramids of apples with names like Gala, Macintosh, Red Delicious, and Pink Lady. I was exhausted with the glory of it all.

At the end of a table, a man whistled while he stacked peaches with loving care into delicate pyramids. When he saw my mother, he nodded.

"Hello, Missus," he greeted her.

I thought my mother blushed a bit. She looked at the floor, smiling, and said nothing. Still, we moved closer to him.

"You're shopping late again." He said this with a kind of sadness and I knew they had talked before. "Is this your daughter?" he asked her.

She moved me toward him with a little pressure on my back but still said nothing.

"Hello, little Missy," he said to me.

Taking my mother's example, I smiled and said nothing as he reached down to lift my hand, giving it a gentle shake.

"Wait a minute," he said, "don't go. Stay right there. I have a surprise for you."

He hurried into the back room, returning seconds later cutting into a peach. The peach had white flesh. I'd never seen that before. My mother held out her hand and the produce man placed a sliver of the peach in her palm. When he held a sliver out to me, I held out my hand.

Of all the miracles that night, this was the best one. The slice of peach melted away on my tongue like sweet butter sprinkled with peach sugar. In the way humans do, I couldn't help but close my eyes, the taste gave me such pleasure. As soon as I swallowed, I opened my eyes again. I wanted to see my mother. She was just laying onto her tongue a second slice. It was like a sacrament; it was like communion. The produce man watched her with glee, his knife poised to provide another slice as soon as that one had disappeared. He had forgotten me as he watched my mother, her enraptured expression, her palm wet with the clear juice of the peach, sweet juice that brought tears to our eyes.

Later, when we walked out into the hot night air again, some of the oppression of it seemed relieved.

"It's like a different country, isn't it?" my mother said. "That's what your father used to say. Just like a different country." We both had the sweet perfume of the white peach lingering in a cloud around us. I can still remember, moments before falling to sleep, licking the last of its sweetness from my lips.

Made in the USA
San Bernardino, CA
02 September 2015